Carin took a deep breath. "What can I do for you?"

It was Nathan's eyes that caught and held her. Blue eyes that had once been soft and loving now glinted like steel as he met her gaze and answered her question.

"Marry me."

Thirteen years ago she would have jumped at the chance. Now Carin forced herself to straighten her fingers, to remain calm, steady, centered.

"No."

It clearly wasn't the answer Nathan had been expecting. He'd shared one night with her; then, consumed by guilt at betraying his brother, he'd told her it was all a mistake! She'd loved him body, heart and soul—and he'd simply disappeared.

Marry him?

Dear Reader

My editor says she has received lots of letters asking, 'Where's Nathan?' from people who have read about his brothers, Rhys and Dominic, in earlier books. My editor herself has asked me, 'Where's Nathan?' more than once.

Nathan, I told her, was out roaming the world. Footloose photographer Nathan Wolfe rarely laid his head in the same place two nights in a row. He didn't have an office, he didn't work nine-to-five. He had no ties that bound him and no interest in creating any. Discovering he was a dad knocked Nathan right off his feet. It made him stop and question everything he'd thought about his life, his family, his past, his present and, ultimately, his future. His future looked suddenly very different. All of a sudden Nathan wanted things he'd told himself he never wanted—a home and a family of his own.

It takes a guy a while to bend his mind around that. That's why, I told my editor, it took Nathan so long to get his book. He had a lot to come to terms with before he could face Carin Campbell again, before he could meet the daughter he never knew he had. But when at last he was ready, he made his move. He came back to Pelican Cay, determined to do the right thing. What Nathan discovered is what most of us discover (what *I* discovered in writing this book)—that life is what happens when you're making other plans.

I hope you enjoy Nathan's story! Thanks for caring about what happened to him!

Anne McAllister

NATHAN'S CHILD

BY

ANNE McALLISTER

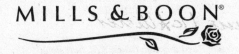
MILLS & BOON®

For my wonderful Aunt Billie!
Sorry you had to wait so long for this!

First published in Great Britain 2003
Harlequin Mills & Boon Limited,
Eton House, 18-24 Paradise Road, Richmond, Surrey TW9 1SR

© Barbara Schenck 2003

ISBN 0 263 83233 3

Set in Times Roman 10½ on 11¼ pt.
01-0503-50811

Printed and bound in Spain
by Litografía Rosés, S.A., Barcelona

CHAPTER ONE

IT WAS A DAY like any other in July on Pelican Cay. It was hot and humid and, according to Trina, the weather girl on the island's on-again, off-again radio station, there was only the faintest hope that a late-afternoon storm would blow in and clear the air.

Carin was grateful for the ancient air conditioner rattling in the window of her small art and gift shop because it kept her cool as she worked, but mostly because its welcome noise brought in customers—day-trippers off the launch from Nassau and week-long vacationers from the local inns and family resorts who came seeking refuge from the sweltering midday heat and lingered because Carin's shop was an island paradise all of its own.

Filled with one-of-a-kind art objects, paintings and sketches, sea glass jewelry, cast sand sculptures and whimsical mobiles that enchanted young and old alike, Carin's Cottage was a haven for those with money and taste and a desire to bring home something more enduring than a T-shirt to remember their holiday by.

Everyone who found their way to tiny Pelican Cay eventually found their way to Carin's. Business was good. Life was sweet.

And she could hardly wait to tell Fiona, the talented but apprehensive young sculptor, that her newest small pieces were headed for Pittsburgh—or would be as soon as Carin finished wrapping them—with the two nice ladies chatting to her about what a lovely place Pelican Cay was.

"Heaven on earth," Carin agreed as she wrapped a small, carved driftwood pelican in blue tissue paper. She put it in a white carrier bag and looked up when the door suddenly opened. She smiled, hoping for another tourist or two before the launch headed back to Nassau.

One look and the smile vanished. "Oh, hell."

The two ladies blinked in astonishment.

"I thought you said heaven," one began.

But the other turned toward the door. "Oh," she said.

"My," she said.

"Who's that?" she said.

"The devil himself," Carin answered under her breath.

"Nathan Wolfe," she said aloud, and was grateful she didn't sound as shaken as she felt.

Nathan Wolfe had always been handsome as the devil. With his thick, black windblown hair and dark tan, he had once been the epitome of male beauty.

The years had honed his looks, sharpened them, hardened them. And now he looked as fierce and hard and predatory as his name as he stood in the doorway of Carin's shop and slowly, behind sunglasses, scanned the room—settling finally on her.

Carin didn't move. Deliberately she stared back, determined to let him know she wasn't afraid of him. Only when she was sure she'd made her point did she avert her gaze, turning back to concentrate on the package she was wrapping for her customers.

They were her priority—not Nathan bloody Wolfe!

But whatever conversation they'd been having before Nathan had opened the door had gone completely out of her head. And the ladies seemed much more interested in Nathan. They stood just drinking in the sight of the hard, devilishly handsome man who looked like nothing so much as a gunfighter just stepping into the OK corral.

"I don't suppose we could buy him," the taller one murmured.

"You wish," the other said.

I wish, Carin thought. And she wished they would take him all the way back to Pittsburgh with them, too.

The taller one studied him a moment longer, but when he didn't seem to even notice her—not once shifting his gaze from Carin—she reached for the bag Carin was filling with their purchases. "Come along, Blanche. We can wrap these back at the ship."

"No," Carin protested hastily. "Don't hurry away. Take your time. Stay awhile." *Stay forever.* If they stayed, maybe Nathan would be the one to leave.

But at that moment he came in and shut the door behind him.

Come on, come on, she thought. *Just get it over with.*

But he didn't move her way. Instead he wandered over to the counter at the far end of the room and began leisurely examining Seamus Logan's coconut carvings, then Fiona's sculptures. Carin gritted her teeth. She watched his easy, nerve-racking grace as he took his time, picking up and studying them all. He moved on then to the handmade toys that the Cash brothers made, Sally's straw weavings, the hand-painted T-shirts and baby rompers that Alisette designed and then he weighed one of old Turk Sawyer's paperweights in his hand.

She'd never thought of Turk's paperweights as weapons before. She did now.

They weren't enemies, she and Nathan. They simply hadn't seen each other in years and years. Thirteen years, to be exact.

And until last September she'd lived in hope of never seeing him again.

But then his brother Dominic had come to Pelican Cay—and Carin had known it was just a matter of time.

But months had passed, and when Nathan didn't come, she began to hope. And now, in the space of a single moment, her hopes had been dashed.

He set the paperweight down and lifted his gaze to study the paintings on the walls—*her* paintings—and with every slow step, Nathan came closer.

Ignoring him as best she could, Carin finished wrapping the last piece of sculpture and put it in the bag. "There you go. I do hope you'll enjoy them—and think of us often. And I hope you'll come back again."

"Oh, we'd love to," one said.

"Especially if you start stocking merchandise like that." The shorter one nodded in Nathan's direction and started for the door.

"He'd be some souvenir," the other agreed with a laugh. Then, eyeing Nathan up and down as she passed, she hurried after her friend. The door opened and banged shut behind them.

In the rattle and hum of the air conditioner, Carin thought she could hear a bomb ticking. She laced her fingers together and took deep, steadying breaths and tried to gather her thoughts—and her defenses.

Thirteen years ago she had been in love with this man. Thirteen years ago he had been gentle, kind, boyish, loving—everything that his hard-edged brother, Dominic, the man she had been engaged to marry, had not.

She'd liked but she hadn't loved Dominic Wolfe. He had been her father's idea of her perfect husband, not hers. But naive girl that she'd been, she'd thought their marriage would work—until she met Nathan.

Knowing Nathan—loving Nathan—Carin had realized that she couldn't marry his brother.

She'd tried to tell Dominic. But he'd told her it was nerves and brushed her aside. She couldn't tell her father— he wanted her marriage to Dominic to cement his business relationship with Dominic's father. Once that had sounded sensible. After she'd met Nathan, she knew it wouldn't be.

So in the end she'd done the only thing she could do— she'd run.

She'd jilted Dominic, had left him at the altar and gone into hiding. She'd been no match for him. He had been too sophisticated, too strong, too handsome, too hard, too powerful for a girl like her.

Ten months ago he'd looked the same. But Carin had grown up a lot in thirteen years. Even so she'd had to muster all her courage to deal with him, to apologize to him—to explain.

And miracle of miracles, he'd changed, too. He'd been kinder, more patient, gentler—a word she'd never imagined using with Dominic Wolfe.

He was married, she'd learned, to the funky, funny purple-haired Sierra, whom she'd met earlier that day. Sierra was the last woman on earth Carin would have imagined with Dominic. But she had obviously been good for Dominic. She'd changed him.

Falling in love had changed him.

Clearly nothing similar had happened to his brother. Nathan looked every bit as fierce and hard and powerful now as Dominic once had. But if she had handled Dominic, she was determined to handle him.

Behind the counter where he couldn't see, Carin smoothed damp palms down the sides of her white slacks. Then she took one last deep breath. ''Good afternoon,'' she said politely in her best shopkeeper's voice. ''What can I do for you?''

Nathan set down the sailboat and slowly turned to face her. The years might have been hard, but they had given him character and even, she noted, a few gray hairs. His formerly straight nose looked as if it had been broken at least once. His tan was still deep and, as she could see when he removed his sunglasses, there were lines at the corners of his eyes.

It was his eyes that caught and held her. Blue eyes that had once been soft and loving now glinted like steel as he met her gaze and answered her question.

''Marry me.''

Thirteen years ago she would have jumped at the chance.

Now Carin forced herself to straighten her fingers, to remain calm, steady, centered.

"No."

It clearly wasn't the answer Nathan had been expecting. His jaw dropped. Then he clamped his mouth shut. A muscle ticked in his temple. He looked equal parts annoyance, consternation and fury.

Well, too bad. Thirteen years ago if he'd said those words to her, Carin would have flung herself on him and wept for joy.

But he hadn't.

He'd shared one night with her, then, consumed by guilt at betraying his brother, he'd told her it was all a mistake! She'd loved him body, heart and soul—and he'd simply disappeared.

Nathan hadn't been there to help her tell Dominic she couldn't marry him. And he hadn't been there nine months later when the fruit of that one night of lovemaking—their daughter, Lacey—had been born.

He was here now, Carin knew, only because Dominic had gone home last autumn and told him about Lacey.

And he'd certainly taken his own sweet time to show up!

Marry him?

She wouldn't have him on a plate.

"No," she said again when he kept standing there as if he was waiting for her to rethink her answer. "Thank you," she added with icy politeness. For nothing.

For a split second Nathan's hard gaze flickered uncertainly. "I would have come sooner," he said gruffly, "if you'd bothered to tell me."

Carin almost snorted. "As if you'd have wanted to know."

They glared at each other. She was gratified when he looked away first.

"What I wanted didn't matter," he said irritably. "I'd have been here if you'd told me."

"You left. Or had you forgotten?"

"You were engaged to my brother!"

"And I'd just made love with you! For God's sake, Nathan, did you honestly think I was going to turn around two days later and marry someone else?"

"How the hell did I know? You were planning to," he argued. "That's what you were there for. You never said you weren't."

"You didn't give me a chance! You practically bolted out of the bed. Then you went running around the house, throwing your stuff in a bag and babbling about what a mistake it had been!"

A deep-red flush suffused Nathan's face. He picked up one of Turk's paperweights, turned it over and over in his hands, then slammed it down and began to pace in front of the counter.

"Okay," he said at last, "I didn't handle it well. It was a new experience for me. I didn't make a habit of sleeping with my brother's fiancées." He turned and leveled a gaze at her. "I didn't know the protocol."

"I don't think there is protocol," Carin said quietly, meeting his gaze levelly. "I think there's just honesty."

The muscle ticked in his temple again. He rocked back on his heels and jammed his hands into the pockets of his jeans. "Ok. Fine. Let's be honest." His voice was harsh. "It was great, but it was wrong. You were engaged, damn it, and not to me! I felt like a heel afterward, and I thought it was in everybody's best interest if I disappeared."

"Is that what you thought?" Carin said with saccharine sweetness. "You thought I'd just forget?"

"I didn't know what the hell you'd do. I barely knew you!"

"You knew me better than anyone in the world."

She'd been so vulnerable that week before the wedding. She'd been so worried. And she'd found in Nathan the kindred spirit she'd always hoped for. She'd poured out her feelings to him—and he didn't believe he'd known her!

Nathan raked his hand through his hair. "I didn't know what you'd do. But believe me, I was shocked as hell to come back to New York five months later and discover you'd jilted my brother and no one knew where you were!"

"You asked?"

"Yes, damn it, I asked."

"And they said they didn't know, and you left it at that." She said the words scornfully.

"What was I supposed to do? You didn't exactly leave a forwarding address. And I sure as hell wasn't going to press the issue. Your whereabouts wasn't Dominic's favorite topic of conversation."

She could believe that. She'd felt guilty for years. Still did. "So, fine. You didn't know where I was. You should have left it at that." She lifted her chin. "Besides, I didn't go anywhere. I was here all the time."

"Hiding out." Nathan said the words dismissively.

"I wasn't hiding out!" she retorted, stung.

"Right. Sent out cards with your forwarding address, did you?"

She looked away.

"And I'm sure all your old friends from Smith and St. Gertrudis or wherever it was you went to school know exactly where you are now. Your father didn't even know!"

"My father didn't want to know."

"What?"

"I called him a week after…after…the wedding didn't…happen. I wanted to explain." It was her turn to shrug now, to act casual, to pretend that what had happened then didn't still hurt. But sadly, whether she wanted to admit it or not, it did. "He didn't want to listen. He told me I was no daughter of his. And then he hung up on me."

"Jesus!" Nathan looked shocked. He paced halfway

down the aisle and scowled furiously. "Nobody told me that."

Carin shrugged. "Maybe no one knew." She couldn't imagine her father had advertised the fact that he had disowned his only child.

Nathan shook his head. "I asked my dad. He didn't know. He just said Magnus said you were okay. That was all. We didn't...talk about it much." Nathan's mouth twisted. "Dominic was...well, not exactly happy."

"I'm sorry." Carin really did regret that. She should have pressed harder that evening before the wedding when he had finally arrived on Pelican Cay and she'd tried to talk to him. She shouldn't have let him brush her off with a grin and an admonition that she'd better go to bed and get her rest because she wouldn't be getting much sleep on their wedding night!

It was that comment, actually, that had made her turn and run.

She couldn't possibly contemplate going to bed with Dominic—making love with Dominic—after her night with Nathan. She *loved* Nathan! There was no way, engaged or not, she could sleep with his brother!

"He seemed...happy..." she ventured "...when I saw him last summer."

"He is. Now."

She winced at the flat accusation in Nathan's tone, but it had the effect of stiffening her spine. "I'm glad," she said. "He wouldn't have been happy with me."

"Because you were in love with me." Nathan didn't look as if he relished saying the words. He tossed them out as if he had to say them, had to confirm them in order to justify his presence here—and his proposal.

"I was twenty-one. A very innocent unworldly twenty-one," she added with a grimace. "A very foolish twenty-one. I've grown up since. I *thought* I loved you. Now I know better."

And if that wasn't entirely honest, it was as close to honesty as she dared to get. She wasn't about to admit that seeing him again had sent her heart somersaulting and that no one but Nathan had ever affected her that way.

It was hormones, she told herself sharply. Sheer animal attraction. Nothing more than a normal response to his male magnetism which, let's face it, Nathan Wolfe still had in spades.

But it was absolutely true—what Carin had said about growing up and knowing better now. It hadn't been love, only infatuation. She'd been enchanted by his dark good looks and his brooding intensity. Mostly she'd been swept away by his enthusiasm, his focus, his dreams and aspirations.

In her circumscribed world all the men she met were like her father—moneyed, high-powered men who ran business conglomerates and whose goal in life was to preserve the family millions and make more. There was certainly nothing wrong with those aspirations, as her father was only too willing to point out to her. His success at achieving them had, after all, paid for their Connecticut estate, their beach house on the cape, her very expensive private school education, and the art and music lessons she'd wanted to take.

Carin knew that. But it had still been refreshing to meet a man who didn't care how many houses he had, who had dropped out of college in his sophomore year and had gone to work on a freighter. That had been the first of many odd jobs. He'd worked as a stringer for a magazine in the Far East, had taken photos on a Japanese fishing boat, had been a deck hand on a copra boat in the South Seas and had washed dishes in exchange for meals and a place to sleep in Chile.

She had listened, wide-eyed and enchanted, to Nathan's tales of a world she had only dreamed about. And he had told her that that's what his life's dream was—to see the world, to experience it, not just read about it...or own it, he'd added disparagingly. He wanted his photos to make it real for people who could never go themselves.

To a young woman who had never had the courage to do what she really wanted to do—who hadn't even *known* what she really wanted to do—Nathan Wolfe had been a hero.

For a week.

Now Carin said firmly, "Trust me, I don't love you now. You don't need to feel any belated compunction to marry me."

"This isn't just about you," Nathan said sharply. "It's about our daughter!"

"*My* daughter. I gave birth to her. I nursed her. I walked the floor with her. I patched up her cuts and bruises and sang her lullabies and read her stories."

"And didn't even tell me she existed!"

"You wouldn't have cared!"

"The hell I wouldn't."

"You left!"

"And now I'm back!"

"Well, we don't need you! So just go away again. Go off to Timbuktu or Nepal or Antarctica. Take your photos. Enjoy your freedom. It's what you wanted!"

"Wanted," he agreed. "Past tense. Like loved."

"What do you mean?" she asked warily.

"I mean it's not what I want now. And I'm not leaving."

She stared at him. "Ever?"

"If that's what it takes." He had the look of his brother again. Hard and implacable. Determined to get his way.

"So you're going to stay here," she said conversationally. "Doing what, If you don't mind my asking?"

"Being a father."

It was the last thing she expected him to say—and it hit her right in the gut. She stared at him. *"You?"*

Kids had never figured in Nathan Wolfe's universe. In

the week they'd spent sharing dreams and hopes and plans, never once had he mentioned wanting a family.

His jaw tightened. "You don't think I can be a good parent?"

"I'm surprised you want to."

"Did you? Want to?"

The question caught her off guard. And the panic she'd felt when she'd discovered she was pregnant appeared unbidden in her mind. She banished it now as she had determinedly banished it all those years ago.

"I always wanted children," she said defensively. "I love my daughter more than anyone on earth."

"I'm looking forward to meeting *our* daughter."

She wanted to say, Well, you're not going to. She wanted to banish him from the island, from her—and Lacey's—life. But she couldn't, and she knew it. He was her daughter's father, and ever since Dominic and Sierra had turned up, Lacey's curiosity about him had been piqued. She'd studied his books avidly, asked a million questions, wondered whether she would ever get to meet him. And Carin had had to smile and act indifferent, as if it wouldn't matter to her whether Nathan appeared or not.

"I'm sure she'll be glad to meet you, too," Carin said stiffly.

"Where is she?"

"Fishing."

Nathan raised a brow. "Fishing?"

"Girls can fish, too."

"I know that. I just didn't think about it. I thought... school or something."

"It's July. No school in July. She went with her friend Lorenzo. He's Thomas's son." Nathan knew Thomas. They were about the same age, and Thomas's parents, Maurice and Estelle, were the caretakers of the Wolfes' house. "They won't be back until late."

Not *that* late actually. Thomas brought his catch in before dinner every day. But Carin wasn't having Nathan hanging around waiting, for the rest of the afternoon.

"I'll just mosey on down to the pier then, shall I?"

"*No!* I mean…no." She'd forgotten Nathan would know that unless a fisherman was going to be gone for several days—in which case he wouldn't be taking a couple of kids—he'd be back in time to sell his catch to housewives looking for fresh fish for dinner. Carin wetted her lips. "You can't just go. I need to talk to her first."

"Come with me. We can talk to her together."

"No. We can't. I can't. I have to keep my shop open." And she didn't want to show up on the quay with Nathan in tow. "Let me talk to her, Nathan. Let me prepare her first. Please."

Nathan jammed his hands into the pockets of well-worn jeans. "Prepare her? How?"

"Tell her that you're here. Have some consideration, Nathan. She thought as soon as you knew about her you'd come. You've known about her for months. You didn't show up until today."

"I had assignments. I had work. I didn't want to come and leave again two days later."

"Fine. Whatever. You did this on your timetable. Give me a chance now."

"All right. You can have the rest of the day."

"But—"

"How long does it take, Carin?" he said impatiently. "Just tell her I'm here. We'll work it out from there."

"We can't—"

"Promise me you'll tell her tonight. Or I'll go down to the pier and tell her myself."

"All right! Fine. I'll talk to her. Tonight," she added grudgingly when he lifted a brow, waiting.

"Do that." He nodded. "And tell her I'll come by to-morrow morning."

She shrugged. "Come whenever you want. You obviously will anyway," she muttered.

Nathan didn't reply He just allowed her a ghost of a smile, then he turned and ambled toward the door. Opening it, he turned back. He leveled his blue eyes on her. "Don't even think of running off."

"As if I would!" she exclaimed hotly.

A corner of his mouth twisted. "See you in the morning," he promised.

To Carin it sounded more like a threat.

So she wouldn't marry him.

Nathan wasn't exactly surprised, since she hadn't even bothered to tell him he was a father! Damn it to hell! He could still get furious just thinking about it! Did she think he wouldn't care that he had a daughter? That he wouldn't have wanted to know?

Even now he could recall the punched-in-the-gut feeling he'd experienced when Dominic had told him he'd met Carin again at Pelican Cay.

Nathan had done his best not to think about Carin Campbell—or the week they'd spent together—for years.

It had been an impossible situation right from the start—the two of them thrown together, more or less alone in the house on the island for an entire week. Nathan, taking a well-deserved vacation from six solid months of being in the field in South America, had shown up at the family house on the island, ready to do his bit as his brother's best man the following Saturday, and had been astonished to find Carin, said brother's quiet, sensitive, pretty fiancée, already there. She'd been sent down early to fulfil a residency requirement for their Bahamian marriage. She'd been there two weeks already—and she'd spent them, as far as Nathan could figure, worrying nonstop about her upcoming nuptials.

"What's to worry about?" he'd asked cavalierly. As

long as it was someone else getting married and not him, he hadn't seen the problem.

But Carin had. Her cheeks had turned a deep-red as she'd admitted, "Your brother."

"Dominic? What's not to like about Dominic? He's handsome, wealthy, powerful, smart." Definitely the best catch of the Wolfe brothers, that was for sure.

"Yes, he is. All of the above," Carin had said faintly. She had barely smiled, and he'd realized she was serious.

He should have realized then she was no match for Dominic. But Nathan had had no experience thinking like an unsophisticated, green girl. Relationships of any sort didn't interest him. Sure, Dominic was hardheaded and used to having his own way, but he was kind, he was honorable, he was the best of men.

"That's the trouble," Carin said when he'd pointed that out. "I don't know anything about men."

"How the hell did you get engaged to him then?"

"Our fathers introduced us."

He should have known. So Dominic was marrying to please their old man. And Nathan supposed Carin was marrying to please hers.

Even so, they had seemed well matched. Both had fathers who were high-powered businessmen, independent entrepreneurs who had used their brains and plenty of hard work to build multinational concerns. Both Dominic and Carin had grown up on the East Coast, had gone to the same sorts of preppy schools and Ivy League colleges, had the same sorts of friends.

And Nathan couldn't imagine that his brother was indifferent to his bride-to-be.

Slender and fine-boned, with long long long blonde hair and wide sea-blue eyes, Carin was your basic, everyday, downright gorgeous female.

If Nathan had been interested in a woman of his own—

which he wasn't—he'd have felt a prick of envy at his brother's lot.

But the last thing Nathan wanted was a wife—especially a wife who would tie him to a corporate lifestyle he had rejected. But Carin was the sort of wife who would suit Dominic to a T. She'd be a terrific accessory to his career and not bad on the home front, either.

So he'd said cheerfully, "You want to learn about men? You want to get to know Dominic? Hell, I'm just like Dominic—" perhaps a stretch of the truth there, but in a good cause "—just stick with me."

He figured they'd have a good time that week. He would enjoy a little friendly platonic female companionship, would cement his role as favored brother-in-law in years to come, and at the same time he'd do Dominic a good turn.

After all, Dominic had gone to bat for him when Nathan had told their father he didn't want to work for Wolfes', that he wanted to be a photographer instead.

The old man had been downright furious. "What do you mean you don't want to work for Wolfes'? It's buttered your bread your whole life, you ungrateful whelp."

Then Dominic had stepped in, pointing out that what Nathan wanted to do was no more than what Douglas had done when he'd built Wolfes' in the first place—be his own man.

"He's the most like you of any of us," Dominic had said forcefully.

Not something Nathan cheerfully acknowledged. But it had stopped the old man. It had made him look thoughtful. And the next thing Nathan knew, his father had been beaming and shaking his hand.

"Chip off the old block," he'd said, nodding his head. "Dominic's right. You've got guts, my boy." He'd fixed Nathan with a level blue gaze. "Fine. Go hop your freighter or thumb your way around the world, if that's what you want. It will be hard and long, but it's your choice."

So Nathan owed Dominic. And showing his wife-to-be a good time and giving her a little confidence had seemed a small chore.

It hadn't been a chore at all.

Carin had been eager to listen to his tales of far-off lands and to ask questions about all his experiences. Very few people, Nathan had discovered, listened as well as she did. He had thoroughly enjoyed basking in her worshipful gaze.

Every day they had gone swimming and snorkeling and sailing. And while they did, he had told her about his family—not only about Dominic, but about their youngest brother, Rhys, and their parents, their mother who had died when they were young, and their father who had been everything to them ever since.

"She taught us to care," he said. "He taught us to be tough."

And Carin had listened intently, taking it all in, nodding and watching him with those gorgeous blue eyes. He told her about the house on the beach out on Long Island where they'd grown up and about the holidays they'd spent here on Pelican Cay when he was a child.

"Dominic has a place in New York," he'd explained. "But only because the offices are there. He isn't as much of a city boy as you might think."

"I don't think he's a boy at all."

Well, no, he wasn't. But Carin wasn't a girl, either. She was a woman.

And Nathan knew it. The more time he spent with her, the greater his awareness of her had grown. His eyes traced the lines of her body. They lingered on her curves. At night it hadn't seemed to matter how much exercise he got during the day, he couldn't settle down, he couldn't sleep. Couldn't stop thinking about her.

She's Dominic's fiancée, he'd reminded himself over and over. And he tried to think about her with his brother, tried to imagine her in bed with Dominic. But his mind left out

Dominic. It only saw Carin. He had fantasies about Carin in bed. And he and not Dominic had been the man in bed with her.

He should have taken off then. Should have started running and never looked back.

He hadn't. He'd stayed. Of course he had stepped up his commentary about Dominic, telling her how his brother had defended his desire to take photos.

But then she'd asked to see them. And when he'd shown them to her, she'd been enchanted, eager to see more, eager to learn about what he looked for in shooting photographs.

And that was when he'd discovered she was an artist.

She'd been shy about admitting it. But when he'd shown her plenty of bad photos he'd taken, she'd relented and allowed him to see her paintings and sketches. They were lively, cheerful, bright, almost primitive paintings and detailed, very realistic sketches. He'd expected something amateurish. Instead she was enormously talented, and he'd told her so.

"What does Dominic think about your work?" he'd asked.

"He wouldn't be interested," she'd said with a shrug. "He only thinks about business."

If he only thought about business when his eager, beautiful, talented fiancée was around, Dominic had rocks in his head.

Nathan hadn't been able to think about anything else.

In fact, whenever he'd thought about the perfect woman for him, Carin was it.

Not that he had said so. He hadn't wanted to make her uncomfortable. Besides, there was no point. Nothing would happen, Nathan had assured himself, because he wouldn't let it.

And possibly nothing would have—if it hadn't been for that storm.

The day before Dominic and his father were to arrive,

Nathan and Carin had gone for a walk after dinner along the pink sand beach. When they'd reached the rocks that jutted out into the sea, he'd held out a hand to help her up, and somehow he'd never let go.

He'd liked holding it, enjoyed running his thumb along the soft smooth flesh, relished the gentle grip she held on his fingers, as if she didn't want to let go, either. It felt right holding her hand. And when they climbed down the other side, their fingers stayed laced together as if by mutual consent. Their hands had known what they were still unable to admit.

When they got back, Nathan remembered telling himself, he would let her go.

The storm had come up quickly, and they were soaked by the time they got back to the house. The wind was chilly, and Nathan had built a fire while Carin changed clothes. Then he'd gone to change his own clothes, expecting to meet her back in the living room and spend the last evening they had together before everyone else arrived lounging in front of the fire.

That's what he'd thought until he'd gone to his room to change. He had stripped down to his shorts when he heard a tap on his bedroom door. "Yeah?"

The door had opened.

Carin had stood before him wearing a towel and a tentative smile. Nothing else. "All my stuff is in the wash and I forgot to put it in the dryer," she confessed. "Do you have some jeans and a sweatshirt I could borrow."

Nathan remembered dumbly nodding his head. He didn't remember saying anything. He didn't think he could have. He'd seen Carin in a bathing suit, of course. He knew— had memorized—those slender enticing curves.

But it was different seeing her wrapped in a towel. It was different knowing that she had nothing on underneath. He remembered the feel of her soft fingers. He wanted to touch the rest of her. His body responded even as his mind tried to resist.

Embarrassed at his sudden fierce arousal, he had turned away toward the dresser. "I'll get 'em," he'd said hoarsely.

But instead of waiting outside his room, she came in. She came to stand beside him—so close that he could see goose bumps on her arms. "You're cold," he'd said. "We've got to warm you up."

He hadn't meant to reach for her. He hadn't meant to make love with her. But the next thing he knew she'd been in his arms.

If he shut his eyes now, Nathan could still remember the tremble of her body against his, could taste her cool flesh as his lips had touched it.

Right here. Right in this room.

Nathan jerked back to the present, cursing the desire that flooded his veins, hating the need that seeing her again this afternoon had aroused!

He grabbed his gear and stamped out of the bedroom. He could sleep in any room. He didn't have to stay in there where the memories would haunt him every second.

But the room next to his had been Dominic's. And Carin had stayed in Rhys's. He stood there, clutching his duffel, torn, frustrated, angry—

And heard a knock on the kitchen door.

He clattered down the stairs, expecting Maurice, who was going to help him build a dark room. "Hey, there," he said, glad for the distraction, as he jerked open the door.

But it wasn't Maurice.

It was a girl.

"Hello," she said politely. "I'm Lacey. You must be my father."

CHAPTER TWO

EVER SINCE DOMINIC had revealed her existence, Nathan had envisioned the day he would meet his daughter, had tried to imagine what he would say to her. And always—every time—their meeting had been at a time and place of *his* choosing.

He'd wanted it to be perfect, knowing full well that, having missed her first twelve years, it never would be.

Still, he'd made an effort.

He'd cleared the decks, finished his assignments, met his commitments. Whenever his agent, Gaby, rang him with new projects, new ideas, new shows, new demands, he turned them down. He wanted nothing on his schedule now but Lacey—and her mother.

He was prepared. Or so he'd thought.

He didn't feel prepared now.

He felt stunned, faced with this girl who wore a pair of white shorts and a fluorescent lime-green T-shirt with the Statue of Liberty and the words New York Babe on it. She had a backpack on her back and sandals on her feet and looked like a hundred preteen girls.

But more than that, she looked like him.

Nathan tried to think of something profound to say or at least something sensible. Nothing came to mind. He had spent much of his adult life in precarious positions—hanging off cliffs, kayaking down white-water rapids, hanging out with polar bears, and tracking penguins in Tierra del Fuego—but none had seemed more precarious than this one.

Now he realized that Lacey was waiting—staring at him,

shifting impatiently from one foot to the other, her hand still stuck out in midair.

Awkwardly Nathan shook it and dredged up a faint grin. "I guess I must be," he said. *Must be your father.*

He felt short of breath. Dazed. Positively blown away. His voice sounded rusty even to his own ears. He stood there, holding her hand—his *daughter's* hand!—learning the feel of it. Her fingers were warm and slender, delicate almost. But there were calluses on her palm. He felt them against his own rough fingers.

From fishing? he wondered. He didn't have a clue. He knew nothing about her. Nothing at all.

She was still looking at him expectantly, and he realized the next move was up to him. "Won't you...come in?"

He felt absurd, inviting his twelve-year-old daughter into his home as if she was a stranger. Fortunately, Lacey didn't seem to see the absurdity of it. She just marched past him into the room, then looked around with interest.

Nathan wondered if she'd ever been in the house before.

He'd always loved it, had thought it was the best place on earth. He had been five when they'd first come to Pelican Cay, and when they'd flown in that first day, he'd thought their little seaplane was landing in paradise. It turned out he wasn't far wrong. Pelican Cay in those days had sand and surf and sun and no telephones to take his father away on business for a week or more at a time.

He and his brothers had spent their happiest hours here. They used to say that it would be the best thing on earth to spend every day on Pelican Cay.

Lacey had. At least he supposed she had.

"Would you...like something to drink?" he asked her. "A soda?" She wouldn't think he was offering her a beer, would she?

"Yes, please." Was she always this polite? Was she always this self-possessed?

He started toward the kitchen, nodding for her to follow.

"Is your…I mean, *where* is your…mother?" Somehow he was sure her visit had not been sanctioned by her mother.

"She teaches a painting class on Mondays," Lacey said. She slipped off her backpack, set it on the counter in the middle of the kitchen. Then she perched on a stool as Nathan opened the refrigerator.

"Pineapple, sea grape or cola?"

"Pineapple, please. It's my favorite."

"Mine, too." Nathan snagged the cans, straightened up and turned around. Their gazes met. And as he popped the tops and handed her the can, they both grinned, sharing the moment and the appreciation of pineapple soda. The knot of apprehension that had been coiled deep and tight inside Nathan ever since he'd discovered he had a daughter suddenly eased.

It reminded him of the feeling he got when he was just beginning fieldwork on a project. The days *before* he was actually there drove him crazy. Once he was involved, he experienced a welcome feeling of relief, a sense of rightness. Like this.

"I'm glad you came," he said, and meant it.

"I'm glad you came," Lacey countered. "I've been needing a father for quite a while."

Nathan's brows rose. "You have?"

"It's difficult to be a one-parent child," Lacey explained. "I don't mean that my mother is a bad mother. She's not. Not at all! She's terrific. And mostly she manages very well. But there are, I think," she said consideringly, "some things fathers are better at."

"Are there?" Nathan was feeling stunned again.

"Mmm. Cutting bait."

He stared at her blankly.

"Fishing." She gave him a despairing look. "You do know how to fish?"

"Of course I know how to fish," Nathan said, affronted.

"I was, um, thinking of something else." As in *fish or...*

"Can't your mother cut bait yet?"

He grinned, remembering Carin's squeamishness when he'd taken her fishing so she would be able to share one of Dominic's pleasures.

"She can. She doesn't like to. She doesn't like to fish."

"And you do." It wasn't a question. He could see the sparkle in her eyes.

"But I always have to go with Lorenzo and his dad, and then Lorenzo always catches the biggest fish."

"Because his dad cuts the bait?"

"No. Because he gets to go with his dad lots more than I do. And we always go where Thomas thinks the fish are biting, and they always are—for Lorenzo."

"I see." Well, sort of, he did. He gathered it had to do with the amount of time Thomas spent with his son—time that Nathan hadn't spent with his daughter. But apparently she wasn't just going to spell it out. Maybe it was the difference between boys and girls.

"Do you know any good fishing places?"

Nathan rubbed a hand against the back of his neck. "I could probably find some." He hoped.

"Good." Lacey took a swallow of her soda. "Lorenzo could come with us, couldn't he?"

"Sure."

"I have your books."

Nathan blinked, surprised by the change of topic, but even more so by what she'd changed it to. "You do?"

Lacey nodded. "My mother got them for me."

"Why?" He could be blunt, too, Nathan decided.

"When I was little I asked about you, and Mom told me you were a photographer. I asked if she had any pictures you took, and she said no. I asked if she could find some. So on my birthday when I was eight, she gave me one of your books. Now I have all of them. They're great."

Nathan didn't know whether to be flattered or furious.

Certainly he was flattered that Lacey approved of his work. But he was also furious that Carin had decided that having his books was all of him that Lacey would need.

"But I like Zeno the best," Lacey said. "Did you live with him?"

Zeno was a wolf. He had been, for want of a better word, the hero of Nathan's last book and in some cases, it seemed, his alter ego, as well. Zeno's "lone wolf" status had been similar to Nathan's own.

"I didn't live with him," he said. "But I spent a lot of time watching him, observing, studying, trying to get to know him."

Lacey bobbed her head. "You did. You knew him. He was my favorite."

"Mine, too." The book itself was called *Solo* and dealt with several years in the life of one young lone wolf. The project had grown incidentally out of an earlier book Nathan had done on Northern wildlife. While there he'd come across a small wolf pack with several young pups. One of them, a young male, often wrestled and played with the others, but seemed more inclined to go off scouting around on his own. Intrigued, Nathan had shot a lot of photos of him.

A year later, when a magazine assignment had taken him back to the same area, he had, coincidentally, happened across the wolves again. The young loner had been an adolescent then, and Nathan had shot more rolls of film of the wolf by himself and interacting with the pack.

After that encounter he'd looked for more assignments in the area, always trying to track down the wolf, who by this time he'd begun to think of as Zeno.

Two years ago he'd simply indulged his desire to learn more by taking the better part of a year to live in the woods up there and study Zeno's comings and goings.

Solo had been published this past spring, the story in text and pictures of one young lone wolf. It had garnered considerable critical praise.

It had also fueled a ridiculous amount of comparison between Nathan Wolfe's own life as a "lone wolf" photographer. He and Zeno were somehow connected in the public's perception.

More than one magazine article had asked, Who would be the woman to settle him down? And it wasn't Zeno they'd been talking about.

By that time, though, Nathan had learned of Lacey's existence, and the question of which woman would "settle him down" had already, to his mind, been decided.

It was just a matter of coming to terms with her—and tying up all the loose ends first.

"Are you going to go back and see Zeno again?" Lacey asked him.

"I don't know."

He had planned to. He'd intended to go there again this summer after he'd finished his other jobs. Gaby had been pushing him to do so. But he'd made those plans last summer, before he'd learned about Lacey. For the moment at least, Zeno was going to have to wait.

"I wish you would," Lacey said. "We gotta know what happens to him."

"Maybe," Nathan said. "But I've got work to do now here."

"You're going to shoot here?"

He shook his head. "I'm writing here. I've done the shooting. Now I have to organize the photos for a book."

"What's it about?"

"Sea turtles."

"Oh." Lacey's expression said she didn't think that would be nearly as intriguing as another book on wolves.

"I got to dive with some," Nathan told her.

"Do you know how to scuba dive? I want to learn to scuba dive. Mom says maybe when I'm older, but it's expensive. Hugh said he'd teach me, but she thinks it would be presuming." Lacey wrinkled her nose. "I don't think Hugh would mind. But as long as you're here…"

"Who's Hugh?"

Lacey giggled. "Hugh the hunk. That's what Mom and Florence call him." Lacey giggled.

"Who's Florence?" Hugh's wife, Nathan hoped.

"Lorenzo's mother."

Not Hugh's wife, then. "So what does this Hugh do, when he isn't scuba diving?" What sort of "hunk" was Carin running around with?

"He runs the charter service. He's got a seaplane and a helicopter and three boats. Last summer when Lorenzo had to have his appendix out, Hugh flew him to the hospital in Nassau. When he came home, Hugh took me along to pick him up. It was way cool. Can you fly a helicopter?"

"No."

"Oh." A pause. "That's too bad." Because maybe she was angling to learn how to fly a helicopter, too? "I used to think maybe he'd be my dad," Lacey said.

Nathan scowled. "Why?"

"Because he likes Mom. An' Mom likes him."

And he was a hunk.

"And now she doesn't?" Nathan hadn't even thought that Carin might have a boyfriend. Dominic had only known that she didn't have a husband.

"'Course she likes him. I told you, he's nice."

"But he's not going to be your dad?"

Lacey gave a long-suffering sigh. "You're my dad," she explained.

"Oh. Right. Of course."

Which was true but wasn't the answer to his question: Does your mother plan on marrying Hugh the hunk? He couldn't bring himself to ask that.

"Do you have your book about Zeno here?" Lacey finished her soda, hopped off the stool, carried the can to the

sink and rinsed it out. "If you do I can tell you my favorite
picture. And you can tell me about when you took it."

"Yeah, I've got it upstairs." He moved to get it. Like a
shadow, Lacey came right after him.

"I like this house," she said, looking around his bedroom with interest. "It's big. Lots bigger than our house."

"Yeah, well, there were three of us boys and my folks."
He opened the duffel on the floor and began pulling clothes
out. There was a copy of each of his books at the bottom.
He'd brought them for Lacey, never thinking Carin would
already have given them to her.

"I've always wanted brothers and sisters." Lacey
perched on the edge of the bed and looked hopefully up at
him.

"Yeah, well, um…brothers are kind of a pain in the
neck."

She gave a little bounce. "Uncle Dominic is really nice.
He came to the shop to see my mom. And then he and
Aunt Sierra were here before Christmas. And he and
Grandpa came down a couple of months ago."

Grandpa?

"Which Grandpa?" Nathan asked warily.

"The only one I've ever met," Lacey said. "Grandpa
Doug."

His *father* had been here? And hadn't even bothered to
mention it?

"Grandpa brought me a camera. Want to see it?"

"A camera? Why'd he bring you a camera?" Nathan
demanded.

"Because he thought it would be good for me to understand your business," Lacey told him.

Yeah, Nathan thought grimly, that sounded like the old
man. Grandkids and business were the two most significant
things in Douglas Wolfe's life. Nathan was almost surprised he hadn't given Lacey a share of the company, and
he said so.

"He wanted to," Lacey said. "My mom said no."

Nathan blinked. That didn't sound like the Carin he remembered. The Carin he remembered wouldn't have said boo to a goose. But then he recalled that she'd taken her life into her own hands the day she'd jilted his brother. So she'd obviously made some changes.

And so had his father if Douglas was taking no for an answer.

"She said if he wanted to visit, he could visit, but he couldn't buy his way into our lives."

Nathan choked back a laugh, imagining his father's reaction to that. Oddly, he felt both proud of Carin for her stance and indignant on his father's behalf. Because he didn't know what to say, he dug through the books in his duffel until he found *Solo*.

"Great." Lacey took it from him and flipped through it confidently, clearly looking for a particular picture. "This one." She laid the book open flat on the bed so they could both look at it.

It was a photo he remembered well. He had taken it across a clearing with a telephoto lens. In the clearing itself, there were three half-grown wolf cubs wrestling with each other. It had been fun-and-games time for them. And that was all most people ever saw, and they cooed and oohed over the frolicking pups.

But now Lacey's finger unerringly found Zeno watching his littermates from behind the brush on the far side of the clearing. He stood silent. Alone. Apart.

"Did you realize," she asked Nathan, "when you took the photo, that he was there?"

"Not at first," he admitted. "I was caught, like anyone would be, at the sight of the other pups. But as I took shot after shot, I really started to look, to focus. And then I saw him there."

"All by himself." Lacey's finger brushed over the Zeno

on the page. "Do you think he was lonely? Do you think he wanted to play, too?"

"Maybe sometimes he did. Sometimes, though, I think he was happier on his own."

"Me, too," Lacey said. "I mean, I'm like that, too." She slanted a glance up at him from beneath a fall of long dark hair. "Are you?"

Nathan considered that, then nodded. "Yeah, I am."

Lacey nodded. She ran her tongue over her lips. "Then…do you think you'll mind being part of us?"

The question caught him off guard.

But before he could even hazard an answer, she went on. "Because I was thinking you might wish you didn't know…about me."

"No," Nathan said flatly. He sat down on the bed beside her and looked straight into his daughter's big blue eyes. "Don't *ever* think that," he said firmly. "Not for a minute. I'm glad I know about you."

Their gazes locked. Seconds ticked by. It was like being weighed and measured, judged for his intentions. And Nathan knew, however long it took, he had to hold her gaze.

Finally a smile spread slowly across Lacey's face. "I'm glad you know about me, too," she said, then sighed. "I didn't think you wanted to."

"Why not?"

"Because you didn't come. After Uncle Dominic and Aunt Sierra were here the first time, I mean."

Nathan looked away, wondering how to explain what he wasn't sure he understood himself. When Dominic had first told him about finding Carin again, he'd been astonished at his reaction. He'd so determinedly "forgotten" her that he was completely unprepared for the sudden clench of his stomach and the flip-flop of his heart at the sound of her name.

And he'd felt awkward as hell about those feelings in

front of his brother. Dominic's old pain was fresh enough
in Nathan's memory to make all his guilt flood back. And
even though Dominic was happy now and glad to understand at last why Carin had jilted him, Nathan hadn't been
able to come to terms with the new circumstances that
quickly.

He'd resisted all thought of renewing his relationship
with Carin.

And then Dominic had mentioned Lacey.

He'd been deliberately vague, mentioning her name casually, hinting at a possibility that had frankly taken
Nathan's breath away.

He had a daughter? He'd been poleaxed by the idea. It
had reordered his reality and had paralyzed him at the same
time. He'd prowled the beach near their Long Island home
for hours afterward, had driven miles. Had tried to think.
But his mind had been a blur.

There was no way he could explain to Lacey the roller
coaster of emotions he'd ridden that night and for weeks
after he'd learned of her existence. A part of him had
wanted to grab the next plane to the Bahamas. A saner,
more rational part had refused to let him.

He needed to get his house in order, to weigh the im-
plications, to decide what would be best for his daughter.
And while he did that, he went on with his life.

He fulfilled the assignments he'd already committed to,
wrote the articles he'd agreed to, took the pictures that
would go in his next book. And all the while—no matter
where he was—his mind was grappling with the knowledge
of his daughter.

"I had commitments," he said finally. "Things that I'd
agreed to do before I knew about you. Photo assignments.
Articles. People were counting on me." *And your mother
definitely was not.* "So I did my job. When I came I wanted
to be ready to stay. I didn't want to have to leave again as
soon as I got here."

Lacey nodded happily. "That's what Grandpa said."

The old man had certainly been sticking his oar in, Nathan thought. But in this instance he was glad. "He was right."

"I'm glad you're staying." She gave a little bounce on the bed. "For how long?"

As long as it takes, Nathan thought. He wasn't sure what the answer was. But he wasn't leaving until he and Carin and Lacey were a family.

"I've got a book to write. Pictures to choose. I'll be doing that here. You can help."

Lacey's eyes lit up. "I can? Really?"

"Well, you can't make all the decisions, but you can have some input. You said you were taking pictures, right?"

"Right. I brought some. An' I brought my camera. They're in my backpack. Want to see them?" She looked eager, and then just a little nervous, as if she might have overstepped her bounds.

But Nathan was delighted. "Of course. Show me."

They went back downstairs and Lacey opened her backpack. Her camera was a good basic single-lens reflex, not a point-and-shoot. Every setting had to be done manually.

"Grandpa said you'd want me to start the way you did," Lacey told him. "Learning how to do everything."

Good ol' Grandpa. It was true, of course. It was exactly what Nathan would have wanted. He handed the camera back to her.

"He said it was exactly the same in business," his daughter informed him. "A person needs to know how to do things herself before she starts taking shortcuts."

"Yeah," Nathan said. "Let's see your pictures."

Lacey hesitated. "I don't focus real good."

"You'll learn."

"And sometimes I wobble a little."

"So do we all."

"And some of 'em are too light and others are too dark."

"It happens. Not every shot is a prizewinner, Lace. I throw out way more than I print."

"Really?" She looked at him, wide-eyed, as if that had never occurred to her. And at his solemn nod, she breathed a sigh of relief and began pulling out envelopes of photographic prints.

Nathan spread them on the island, and they pulled up stools and sat side by side, looking at them. She was right—many of them were out of focus, many were too dark or too light. On some the camera had clearly wobbled. But she had a nice sense of composition. She had an eye for telling detail.

There were pictures of the harbor and the village, of Maurice blowing a conch shell to call the women to buy fresh fish, of Thomas, Maurice's son and the father of Lacey's friend Lorenzo, cleaning fish on the dock. There were lots of pictures of a boy Lacey's age, mugging for the camera, walking a fence like a tightrope, sitting astride one of the old English cannons near the cliff. Lorenzo, no doubt.

There was a particularly well-composed picture of a row of colorful shirts flapping on a clothesline in the wind and, behind them, a row of pastel houses climbing the hill, their colors pale echoes of the flapping shirts.

Nathan edged that one away from the others. "This is really strong."

Lacey's eyes lit up. "You think?"

"Oh, yeah."

More confident now, she pulled out more envelopes from her backpack and opened them up. Suddenly Nathan found himself staring at Carin.

Close-ups of Carin looking stern, looking pensive. Laughing. Rolling her eyes. Sticking her tongue out at the camera. Long shots of Carin walking on the beach or sitting on the sand or working in her shop.

And a particularly wonderful one of Carin on the dock, her feet dangling in the water, as she turned her head and looked up at her daughter and smiled.

It was a smile Nathan remembered, a smile that, deep in his heart, he had carried with him for the past thirteen years. It was the smile she'd given him so often that week they'd spent together, an intimate, gentle smile that touched not just her mouth but her eyes, as well.

For years, in his wallet, he'd carried a picture of that smile. The photo, one he had taken during their week together on the beach, had become worn from handling and faded from exposure to all kinds of weather. Two years ago he'd had his wallet stolen in a street bazaar in Thailand. The inconvenience of having to get his driver's license reissued and his credit cards changed was annoying. But the loss of that photo more than anything had left him feeling oddly hollow and alone.

Now, unbidden, his fingers went out and touched the one Lacey had taken.

"It's the best one, isn't it?" she asked.

"It's...very good. The way the light..." His voice trailed off because his reactions had nothing to do with the way the light did anything.

It was all Carin. He picked it up and stared at it. She could have smiled at him like that today. She could have thrown her arms around him, welcomed him...

"You can have it if you want," Lacey offered.

"No, that's okay." Hastily he set it back down, steeling himself against an ache he refused to acknowledge. He felt trapped suddenly, cornered by emotions he didn't want to face.

He shifted from one bare foot to the other, then drummed his knuckles nervously on the countertop. "Well, those are good," he said briskly, gathering the Carin photos into a pile and tucking them firmly back into the envelope. "Let's see what else you've got."

But before Lacey could pull out any more envelopes, there was a knock on the front door.

"That'll be Maurice. I can talk to him later."

But he was wrong again.

It was Carin, pacing on his porch. When he opened the door she whirled to demand, "Where's Lacey?" Her voice was high and shrill, like nothing he'd ever heard from her before.

"She's, uh…I—"

"*Where is she?*" She pushed past him. "Lacey!" She strode into the living room, looking around wildly. "Lacey Campbell! Where are you?"

"She's in the kitchen. Cripes, Carin, relax. She's—"

"I'm here, Mom." Lacey appeared in the doorway, clutching her backpack, looking worried.

"See," Nathan said. "She's fine."

But Carin didn't even look at him. She was glaring at their daughter. "I told you he was coming by tomorrow, didn't I?"

"Yes. But I wanted to see him tonight."

"And the world runs according to what you want?"

"I left you a note."

"Not good enough."

"I'm almost thirteen years old!"

"Then start acting like it."

"*He* was glad I came. Weren't you?" Lacey turned to him.

Shoved straight into the middle, Nathan swallowed. "Of course. But—"

"See!" Lacey said triumphantly to her mother.

Carin shot him a fulminating glare. "It doesn't matter whether he was glad or not. I'm your mother and I didn't give you permission."

"Well, he's my father and he—"

"Doesn't want you to start a fight with your mother," Nathan said firmly, getting a grip at last. If there was one thing he did know about parenting it was that the two of them needed to present a united front. "I was glad to see you," he said to Lacey. "Very glad. But glad as I was, if your mother said tomorrow, she meant tomorrow. You shouldn't have come without asking."

"But—"

Nathan steeled himself against the accusation of betrayal in her look. "It might be tough being a one-parent child," he told her firmly, "but you'll find out it's not always a picnic having two, either. Especially when they stick to-gether."

Lacey scowled. She looked from him to Carin and back again. Her shoulders slumped.

Nathan hardened his heart against it. "Go on with your mother now," he said, feeling every inch the father Carin had never given him a chance to become. "I'll see you tomorrow."

"But—" She turned beseeching eyes on him.

"Tomorrow, Lace. Unless you don't want me to show you that fishing spot."

Lacey's eyes narrowed, as if she weren't sure she be-lieved him. She waited hopefully for him to cave in. When he didn't, she shook her head sadly. "You're as bad as Mom," she muttered. Then, shouldering her backpack, she loped past him out the door.

Watching her go, Nathan felt guilty and parental at the same time. He supposed it was a fairly common feeling. Once Lacey had gone, he looked at Carin.

Her arms were crossed like a shield over her breasts. "Thank you," she muttered, her tone grudging.

"Don't fall all over yourself with gratitude."

"Don't worry. I won't."

Her intransigence annoyed him. "Oh, come on, Carin. No harm done. She's fine. And you can hardly blame her for wanting to meet me."

Carin's eyes flashed. "I blame her for not following the rules!"

"I remember when we didn't always follow the rules, Carin."

Their gazes met. Locked. Dueled. Minds—and hearts—remembered.

"Carin—" He tried once more, said her name softly this time.

But she tore her gaze away. "Good night, Nathan."

And she hurried down the steps and almost ran up the drive after their daughter.

CHAPTER THREE

"HE'S SO COOL, Mom," Lacey said over and over as they walked home.

As soon as she was sure that her mother wasn't furious anymore, Lacey hadn't stopped singing Nathan's praises. All the way over the hill and along the narrow road through the trees and into Pelican Town she chattered on.

"He told me about Zeno. The wolf Zeno," Lacey qualified, because the mongrel dog she had taken to feeding a few months back and who now slept on the porch was, amazingly enough, called Zeno, too.

"Did he?" Carin responded absently.

"And he liked my photos! He said they were good. Did you know he has to throw out a lot of his, too?" Lacey hopped around a pothole and grinned over her shoulder at her mother. "He says he throws out way more than he keeps."

"I'm sure that's true."

She wasn't really listening to her daughter. She was busy cringing at how frantic she'd sounded and feeling furious that he had sided with her so willingly—even though, she acknowleged, she'd have been even more furious if he hadn't.

"He even said I could help him pick photos for his next book." Lacey opened the gate to their tiny front garden. "D'you want to see which ones of mine he really liked?"

"Tomorrow," Carin said.

"But—"

"Tomorrow, Lacey," Carin said in her she-who-must-be-obeyed voice. "Go get ready for bed. It's nearly eleven o'clock."

She could see that Lacey was humming with energy and the desire to talk till dawn. But Carin needed peace and quiet and she needed them now. Apparently, one look at her face and Lacey must have figured that out. Heaving a theatrical sigh and grumbling under her breath, her daughter went up the stairs.

Carin sank onto the sofa, stared at the slowly whirling ceiling fan, drew a deep breath and felt the adrenaline fade. She was spent, frazzled, completely shot.

Was this what having Nathan back in her life was going to do?

Dear God, she hoped not.

She'd thought she was ready to deal with him. But she hadn't expected this.

The Nathan she'd expected would have railed at her about not telling him about Lacey, but would actually have been relieved that she hadn't. He would have gruffly offered her financial assistance, would have complimented her on how well she had raised their daughter, and would, after a few hours—or at the most, a few days—have taken off for parts unknown.

That Nathan she could have dealt with.

This Nathan made her nervous.

This Nathan seemed both implacable and reasonable. She'd expected Lacey to be charmed by him. What woman between the ages of three and ninety-three wasn't?

But she hadn't expected him to plan to take their daughter fishing!

Of course she was sure it had been Lacey's idea. But Nathan would enjoy it. They would bond.

Hadn't she herself bonded with him under similar circumstances? Carin remembered well the times he had taken her fishing. His quiet competence and serene enjoyment out on the water had put her at her ease, and his patience as he taught her everything she needed to know had calmed her at the same time it had caused her to fall even deeper under his spell.

It was his patience that worried her now.

What if he really did intend to stick around? What if she had to see him day after day, week after week?

Dear God. It didn't bear thinking about.

Lacey finished brushing her teeth, and Carin heard the floorboards squeak as her daughter crossed the hall to her bedroom, so she climbed the stairs to act sane and sensible and calm and maternal—and hope she convinced Lacey even if she didn't convince herself.

Lacey was in bed, covers tucked up to her chin. Carin hoped she wasn't going to start in again on how wonderful Nathan was.

She didn't. She said instead, ''I was afraid he wasn't going to come.''

All the bounce was gone now. This was the reflective Lacey. Usually her daughter was eager, cheerful and fearless—much more outgoing than Carin, so that sometimes she forgot that Lacey had insecurities, too. Sometimes it seemed as if she didn't.

Now she realized that Lacey might just be better at masking them. Lacey wasn't one to talk about her fears, and she'd certainly never before confided this concern about her father. She'd asked lots of questions about Nathan—especially since Dominic had appeared last year—but she'd never seemed to fret about him.

Carin had been apprehensive, of course, when she'd had to introduce Lacey to Dominic. But the two of them had hit it off quite well. And while Lacey had asked questions about her father and his family after meeting Dominic and Sierra and, later, Douglas, she'd never asked, ''When's my father coming to see me?''

Carin had been pleased and relieved, convinced that Lacey simply hadn't cared enough to ask. Now she realized that the really important questions might be the ones Lacey didn't ask. Her heart squeezed just a little.

"Would it have mattered so much?"

Lacey levered herself up on her elbows. "Of course it would matter! He's my father! I want to know him. I've *always* wanted to know him!"

The ferocity of her tone cut Carin to the bone. It challenged the most basic decision she'd made—not to tell Nathan about their child.

And yet she knew, given the same circumstances, she would do the same thing again. Given who Nathan was and what he wanted to do with his life, she'd had no choice.

He might think differently now. He might blame her now. But thirteen years ago, keeping her pregnancy a secret had been the right thing to do. If she'd told him, she'd have effectively tied him down to a life she knew he'd hate, to obligations he hadn't chosen. If she'd told him, he might have married her.

But he would never have loved her.

He *hadn't* loved her, even when they'd made love.

She made herself reflect on that for a long moment because that had been the other fact on which she'd based her decision. Even when she'd found out she was pregnant, she knew she couldn't have begged Nathan for marriage—not when she'd given him her heart and he'd only shared his body. It would have destroyed them both.

In the end there had been only one thing to do. And the truth was, she admitted to herself, she had barely considered Lacey's needs at all.

Later she'd assured herself that it would be better for Lacey to have one parent who loved her than have two where one of them might resent her very existence.

Now Carin took a careful, steadying breath and let it out slowly.

"Well, he's here now," she said with far more calm than she felt as she smoothed the light cotton blanket over

Lacey, then bent to give her daughter a kiss. "So you can enjoy getting to know him."

"I will," Lacey vowed, and settled back against the pillows again.

On a normal night, once Lacey had gone to sleep, Carin would have finished up her bookwork from the store, then made herself a cup of tea and taken it out on the porch to sit in the swing and unwind from the day.

Tonight she couldn't settle. She tried to do her bookwork and couldn't concentrate. She made a cup of tea and couldn't sit still to drink it. She paced around the house, picking things up and setting them back down again.

Finally she went outside and flung herself down on the swing, grabbed her sketchbook and tried to funnel some of her restless energy into ideas for her work. But all her drawings became sharp-featured, dark-haired men, and she ripped them out of the sketchbook, crumpled them up and tossed them aside, wishing it were as easy to get rid of Nathan.

A creaking noise at the gate made her look up. A pair of yellow eyes glinted in the darkness. "Ah, Zeno," she said as the gate was nosed further open. "Come here, boy."

A dark shape shambled toward the porch. He was a little taller than an Irish setter, a little wirier than a terrier, a little more spotted than a dalmatian, a little less mellow than a golden retriever. He had turned up one day, full-grown, and no one knew which visiting boat he'd come off.

Her friend Hugh McGillivray, who ran Fly Guy, the island transport company, had begun calling him Heinz because he was at least fifty-seven varieties of dog. But Lacey had named him Zeno because he had appeared on their doorstep about the same time Nathan's book, *Solo,* had come out.

"He looks nothing like a wolf," Carin had protested.

"Looks aren't everything. Are they, Zeno?" Lacey had

said stubbornly, hugging the gangly animal who had grinned and furiously wagged his tail.

"He's not ours to name." Their house wasn't close to big enough for a dog the size of a wolfhound.

"He's nobody else's," Lacey rejoined practically. "Not unless someone comes back for him. Besides," she added, apparently deciding that an outside dog was better than no dog at all, "he doesn't have to come in. He can just come around."

Which was pretty much what he did. Zeno the dog seemed to have no more interest in settling in any one place than Zeno the wolf had. He moved from place to place, from house to house—life was a movable feast for Zeno—and pretty soon everyone on the island knew him, fed him and called him by the name Lacey had given him. Mostly he divided his time between their place and Hugh's, because Hugh had a mostly border collie called Belle who had apparently caught Zeno's eye.

Tonight, though, Belle must have had other plans as Zeno was looking hopefully at Carin. She scratched his ears and rubbed under his chin. It was soothing, petting the dog. It calmed her, centered her, slowed her down.

"Thanks for coming," she told him with a wry smile.

Zeno grinned. His tail thumped on the porch. He looked toward the door. Carin knew what he wanted.

"It's late," she told him, "You must have eaten. Didn't Hugh feed you? What about Lorenzo?"

But Zeno cocked his head and whined a denial.

Carin sighed and rolled her eyes. "Okay, fine. Let me see what we've got." Giving his ears one last scratch, she went inside to check the refrigerator. She found leftover peas and rice from dinner plus a bit of the fish Lacey had caught. Carin crumbled it into a bowl, carried it back through the living room and started to push open the screen door.

"Here, Zee—"

Nathan was on the porch.

So much for calm and settled. Carin's fingers automatically clenched the bowl in her hand. Instead of going out, she let the screen bang shut between them. "What are you doing here?"

"We need to talk."

"No, we don't."

"Yes, we do. Invite me in or come out here."

Zeno, whining at the sight of the bowl, offered his opinion.

Nathan reached for the door handle.

Carin beat him to it. "Fine. We'll talk out here." She yanked the door open and stalked past him onto the porch. Zeno pushed between them, his eyes fixed on the bowl, his tail thumping madly.

Nathan reached down and absently scratched his head. "Who's this?"

"A dog."

"No? Really? I'd never have guessed." Sarcasm dripped. "What's his name?"

Carin didn't want to say, knowing full well what he'd think. But if she didn't, Lacey undoubtedly would. "Zeno," she said defiantly. "Lacey's choice."

A corner of his mouth lifted. "Somehow I didn't imagine it was yours."

"He turned up about the same time your book did." She put the bowl down so that Zeno would have to stay between them to eat. Then she straightened up again, wrapping her arms across her breasts as if they could protect her.

"I was surprised Lacey had read my books."

Carin shrugged. "She was curious."

"About them or about me?"

"About what you did. Your job." She turned away from him and stared out into the darkness. Down the hill she could hear the faint sounds of steel drum music coming from the Grouper Bar and Café. The night breeze, which normally she looked forward to, seemed chilly now, and Carin rubbed her bare arms to ward off goose bumps.

"She seems interested," Nathan said after a moment.

"I guess." She still didn't look his way, but she didn't need to in order to know he was there, right on the other side of Zeno. It was almost magnetic, the pull he had over her. She'd never felt that way about any other man. She didn't want to feel that way about this one. Didn't want to fall under his spell again.

"What do you desperately need to talk to me about?" she said when he didn't speak.

"Lacey. Fishing. This parenting bit. How we're going to handle it."

"I handle this 'parenting bit' just fine, thank you."

"Good for you. But you're not handling it alone anymore. There are two of us now. And you're going to have to remember that. We need to present a united front. We don't argue in front of our daughter."

"Don't tell me how to parent!"

"I backed you up tonight."

"I said thank you."

"And I'll expect the same from you when I tell her something."

"If I agree with you, I will."

"Whether you agree or not," Nathan said evenly.

"No way! If you think you can just waltz in here and take over and expect me to back you up—"

Nathan lifted a brow. "Like you took over and never even told me we had a child?"

"You wouldn't have wanted—"

"You didn't let me decide what I wanted!"

"So I'm the bad guy in this? I'm the one everybody blames?" Carin said bitterly.

First Lacey, now Nathan. As if she'd taken on single parenthood for thirteen years to spite them both.

"You're not the bad guy, Carin," Nathan said gruffly.

"I'm sure you did what you thought was the right thing at the time."

She snorted. "Thank you very much for the vote of confidence."

"Jesus, what is it with you? I'm trying to give you the benefit of the doubt!"

"Don't bother."

He drew a breath, then let it out and sighed. "Look, Carin. I didn't come here tonight to fight with you. And I didn't come to Pelican Cay to make your life miserable. I came because my daughter's here."

If Carin had ever dared hope he'd come back for *her*, she knew now that she'd hoped in vain. It was only Lacey he'd come for.

She swallowed the hurt, told herself it didn't matter, that she wasn't surprised. Which she wasn't.

"And you're determined to do your duty by her." Her tone was mocking. She couldn't help it.

"Yes, damn it, I am."

"Bloody noble of you. And unnecessary. We don't need you."

"Lacey does. She said so."

Hell. Oh, hell.

"Well, *I* don't need you. And I don't want you!"

"Don't you?"

His quiet challenge made her glare at him in fury. "What are you saying?"

"That once upon a time, you damned well wanted me!" And he stepped around Zeno, who never even looked up as Nathan hauled her into his arms and kissed her.

It was a kiss to remember—a kiss so like the passionate kisses they'd shared so long ago that it was as if all the years between vanished in an instant. As Nathan's hot mouth pressed hers, persuaded hers, opened hers, Carin's mind fought the surge of desire, the onslaught of memory. But her body did not.

Her body wanted it—wanted him.

For years she'd told herself she had imagined the hunger in the kisses they'd shared. For years she'd almost believed it.

But it wasn't true. She hadn't exaggerated. This kiss was as fierce and possessive and hungry as his long-ago kisses had been. And it touched that same chord deep inside her, and she responded. Desire and need and hunger and passion all resonated, reverberated, began to grow.

Blood pounded through her veins, her heart hammered against the wall of her chest. And against her will, against her better judgment, against everything she had been telling herself for years, she opened to him. Her lips parted, savored, welcomed.

And then, heaven help her, she was kissing him back.

Nathan groaned. "Yesss." The word hissed between his teeth, and he wrapped his arms around her more tightly and pressed his hard body against hers. And far from frightening her away, the pressure of his arousal incited and encouraged her own. Her own hunger, unsatisfied for so long and now awakened, was ravenous. She deepened the kiss, couldn't stop herself, needed it, needed *him!*

And then quite suddenly, Nathan wrenched himself away.

Carin stared at him, stunned, the night breeze cold on her burning flesh.

"There," he said raggedly, "I'd say that pretty much proves it." His breathing came quick and harsh. The skin over his cheekbones was flushed and taut.

Dazed, Carin shook her head. "Proves what?" She ached, abandoned and bereft.

"I said you wanted me once, Carin. You still do. We'll start from there."

"So," the gruff voice on his cell phone said the minute Nathan answered it. "When's the wedding?"

"Dad?"

Douglas Wolfe was the last person Nathan expected to hear when he'd grabbed the phone off the bedside table. And yet, the moment he heard his father's unmistakable baritone, he didn't know why he was surprised.

Just because the old man had never rung him on his cell phone before—and as far as Nathan had known, didn't even have his number—didn't mean that Douglas wouldn't have it and use it when he chose to.

"Of course it's me. Who were you expecting?" Douglas gave a huff of impatient indignation. "So, did you set the date?"

How his father even knew he'd proposed was a mystery to Nathan. But Douglas Wolfe hadn't run an internationally respected company for thirty years by being unaware. He had tentacles everywhere.

"The old man's an octopus," Dominic had once said, a note of respect and awe in his voice.

Nathan hadn't given a damn then about his father's far-reaching tentacles; they'd had nothing to do with him. Now they did. He raked a hand through his hair, wondering if the old man had the house bugged or if he could just read minds.

If so, he ought to try reading Carin's.

"No," Nathan said flatly. "We didn't set a date."

"Why the hell not? You dallied around a whole year just getting down there."

"I had obligations."

"You have a daughter!"

"I know that," Nathan said roughly. "And I didn't want to come and have to leave again right away. I took care of my responsibilities elsewhere, and now I'm here. I spent this evening with my daughter."

"Ah, you met her? Isn't she a peach?" Douglas's whole tone changed, and Nathan could hear his father's obvious delight. "Pretty as a picture. Reminds me of your mother."

There was just a hint of wistfulness in his father's tone as the older man recalled Nathan's mother who had been the love of his life. "Beth would have loved her," Douglas said. "She's smart as a whip, too, that girl. Got a good head on her shoulders. Polite, too. Wrote me a thank-you letter after I, er, stopped to see her in the spring." He said that rather quickly, as if he wasn't sure he ought to be admitting to having visited his granddaughter.

"She showed me the camera you gave her," Nathan said so his father would know he was aware of the visit. "Thanks."

"Made sense to give her one," Douglas said briskly. "She was interested."

"She's taken some pretty nice shots."

"Figured she might. Reckon she comes by it naturally, what with you being a photographer and her mother an artist." Douglas paused again. "That Carin's got talent."

"Yes."

Douglas waited for him to amplify. He didn't.

Finally, impatiently, Douglas demanded, "So when *are* you going to set the date? Dominic will need to know in order to set aside some time, and Rhys will have to apply for leave."

"Sorry. Can't help you."

"What's that supposed to mean? By God, boy, she had your child. I don't care if thirteen years has gone by, Lacey is a Wolfe!"

"I know that!"

"Well then, do your duty and ask—"

"I asked." The words hissed through Nathan's teeth. "She said no."

The sputterings of disbelief on the other end of the line should have been comforting. Dominic, Nathan was sure, would have been heartened to know the old man was on his side. And even their younger brother, Rhys, wouldn't have seen Douglas's meddling as a liability.

Only Nathan had consistently turned his back on their father's commands. He hadn't finished college. He hadn't gone into the family business. He hadn't shown any interest in any of the girls Douglas had wanted him to date. Instead he'd taken his camera and left. He'd made his own way in the world ever since.

It had been a point of pride to do things his own way.

And in the old days he would have taken Douglas's demand that he marry Carin as reason enough to pack his bags and head for the hills. Even now Nathan found that the instinct ran deep.

But for once, unfortunately, he agreed with his father's assessment of the situation. He was Lacey's father and he wanted to be part of her life. More than a peripheral part.

Easier said than done.

"She said no?" Douglas was still sputtering. "I'll talk to her," he said.

As if that would help. Nathan was almost tempted to say, Be my guest.

He could just imagine how Carin would react to Douglas's corporate power tactics. She'd run from them once already when she'd jilted Dominic.

There was nothing to stop her running again.

But having seen her today, Nathan didn't think she'd run this time. The Carin Campbell he'd met today wasn't merely older, she was stronger. She wasn't a girl anymore. She was a woman. There was a resilience and a determination in the grown-up Carin that she'd lacked all those years ago. She had no trouble speaking her mind now.

He had no doubt she'd speak it to Douglas if he attempted to interfere, too. And Nathan didn't need any more complications than he already had.

"You stay out of this," he told his father.

"I'm only trying to help." Douglas sounded aggrieved.

"Fine. Then don't meddle. Leave us alone."

"Left you alone for a year."

Nathan ground his teeth. "And you'll keep on doing it now. Trust me, Dad, you sticking your oar in won't help at all."

"She likes me. Said so. Said it was good for Lacey to know me. Told me I could come and visit anytime. I could just sort of drop in and—"

"No!" Nathan said sharply. He drew a steadying breath. "No," he said again, more moderately. "Thank you. I appreciate the support, but I'll handle it."

Douglas didn't say anything for a long moment. Then he sighed. "I damned well hope so."

To be honest, Nathan did, too.

CHAPTER FOUR

WEDNESDAYS were Carin's day to paint.

Last month she had promised Stacia, her agent, a dozen more paintings for the show Stacia had got her in New York City right before school started. That meant a lot of hard work.

So every Wednesday Fiona Dunbar did behind-the-counter duty while Carin stayed home and painted.

But that wasn't going to happen today.

Fiona had arrived, of course, bright and early to pick up the cash box and anything else Carin wanted to send to the shop. She was standing in the kitchen, drinking a cup of coffee and talking animatedly about the collection of flotsam and jetsam she was going to use for her next big sculpture, when Carin heard a noise on the porch and turned to see Nathan at the screen door.

This morning he wore a pair of faded denim jeans and a chambray shirt with the tails flapping. His sunglasses were parked on top of his thick, tousled hair, and Carin thought he looked like an ad for Ray●Bans, gorgeous as ever and well rested to boot.

Clearly he hadn't tossed and turned all night. The kiss that had kept her awake for hours obviously hadn't affected him!

But then, it wouldn't, would it? He didn't love her.

Well, damn it, she didn't love him, either, Carin vowed. Not anymore. She steeled herself against reacting to him now.

Fiona had no such compunction. Always a connoisseur of male beauty, Fiona gave Nathan an appreciative once-over and murmured, "Well now, where'd you find him?"

"He's here to pick up Lacey."

Fiona stared. "*Lacey?* Since when is Lacey going out with gorgeous guys old enough to be her father?"

"He is her father."

Fiona's jaw dropped. "That's Lacey's *father?* That gorgeous...I didn't know Lacey's father was coming," she said accusingly.

"Neither did I." And she wouldn't have announced it in any case. "Lacey will be right back," she said to Nathan, not bothering to invite him in. "She went to borrow some fishing gear from Thomas."

"Good." He didn't wait for an invitation. He stepped into the kitchen and smiled at Fiona, who looked at Carin expectantly.

"Aren't you going to introduce us?"

Carin introduced them. Fiona didn't only admire his looks, she was disgustingly flattering about Nathan's photos and his books and articles and how pleased she was to meet him. And Nathan was his most charming, too, saying he'd noticed Fiona's sculptures in Carin's shop. He'd thought they were eye-catching and appealing—even the weird ones made out of stuff Fiona had found on the beach. They were well on their way to forming a mutual admiration society when Lacey at last appeared.

"Hey, wow! You're early." She beamed when she saw Nathan already there. "I got some stuff from Thomas." She waggled the rod, coming dangerously close to decapitating Fiona. "I thought I'd bring my camera, too. So I can take pictures. And maybe afterward you could show me some of yours?"

"Don't pester," Carin warned Lacey, who seemed about ready to offer yet another suggestion.

"I never pester," Lacey said indignantly. "All set?"

Nathan nodded. "All set."

They started out the door.

"Wait." Carin snagged Lacey's neon-lime-green ball

cap off the hook by the door and thrust it at her daughter. "And don't forget sun screen."

"I won't." Lacey rolled her eyes.

"And wear your life jacket. You do have life jackets?" Nathan nodded.

"And don't stand in the boat and—"

"If you're so worried that we can't manage without you," Nathan cut in, "why don't you come along, too."

"No! Thank you. I have work to do."

"Mom paints on Wednesdays," Lacey said. "She's got a lot to do 'cause she's having a show."

Nathan's brows lifted. "A show? Where?"

"In New York City," Lacey said proudly.

The brows hiked even further. He looked at Carin for more details.

She shrugged. "It's no big deal."

It was a huge deal, and sometimes she thought she'd made a mistake agreeing to it. A successful one-woman show in New York City would take her to a whole new level. She'd had a couple of shows in Nassau and one in Miami. But Stacia hoped to broaden her market.

But if the critics panned her work or the sales weren't there, Carin knew she would regret it. She had agreed to the show only because the offer had come after Dominic had discovered her whereabouts. There was no longer any point in keeping a low profile. And she'd hoped that the show would result in more money in case she needed to fight Nathan in court.

She didn't imagine she would have to—couldn't believe he would want custody of Lacey—but it would be better to have a nest egg than not.

"Where?" Nathan asked now.

She told him. It was just a small gallery in Soho. But he'd heard of it.

"I'll have to go," he said. Which would be fine with her because she had no intention of going.

"Dad," Lacey said impatiently. It amazed Carin how she

could say the word so easily, as if she'd been saying it all her life.

"Coming," Nathan said just as easily. "You won't mind if I don't bring Lacey back until after dinner, then? Since you're going to be painting all day."

Hoisted by her own petard. Carin pressed her lips together. "Fine. If that's what you want."

"It's what we want, right, Lace?" Nathan took the ball cap Lacey held and clapped it on her head. "Come on, kid. We've got dinner to catch."

Giggling and grinning over her shoulder at her mother, Lacey followed her father out the door.

"Wellllllllll," Fiona said when the door shut after them, "I can certainly see why you went to bed with him!"

Carin flushed. "I was young and foolish and it was a mistake. Except for Lacey."

"Of course." Fiona nodded, then slanted Carin a glance. "You had very good taste. He's lovely."

"It's purely skin deep," Carin said. Of course that wasn't entirely true, but she was not getting into a discussion about what had attracted her to Nathan in the first place.

"The bones aren't bad, either," Fiona said with a grin, "speaking as a sculptor, of course. Still got the hots for him?"

"Of course not!"

Fiona's grin turned wicked. "Protesting just a bit too much?"

Carin clamped her mouth shut.

Fiona added a little more coffee to her cup and settled against the kitchen cabinet. "When did he show up?"

"Yesterday." Pointedly Carin glanced at her watch. "I think you might want to head on over to the store. Turk brought paperweights by yesterday. You can price them and put them out in a display."

"Okay." Fiona nodded, sipping her coffee. "How long's he staying?"

Carin sighed. "Who knows? Who cares? Tommy Cash is supposed to be bringing some toys into the shop this morning. You'd better get a move on."

"You'll feel better if you talk about it."

"I'll feel better if you go open my shop and I can get to painting!"

Fiona tut-tutted. "So testy this early in the morning."

"I've got work to do."

"Fine." Fiona took one last swallow of coffee and poured the rest down the sink. "If you ever want to talk about it. About *him*—"

"I will certainly let you know," Carin said. Not. "Now I really have to get to work. I need eight more paintings at least."

Fiona picked up the box of paperweights and, shaking her head at Carin's one-track mind, pushed her way out the screen door. "Down, Zeno."

He was waiting on the porch, angling for breakfast. But when Carin shut the screen again, he followed Fiona toward the gate.

"I'll bring you a sandwich for lunch," Carin called after her. "Ham or grouper?"

"Ham." Fiona opened the gate. Zeno, spying Carin's neighbor's cat, forgot all about breakfast and shot through the gate after it. The cat took one look, darted under the fence and hid. Zeno barked, paced, prowled, hovered.

Ordinarily Carin found his antics amusing. This morning, feeling hunted herself, her sympathies were all with the cat.

She took a cup of coffee with her and went out back to her tiny studio. She had three paintings in varying stages of progress. She had twenty or thirty sketches that she should be working from.

She started to work on a painting of some children playing on the quay. But the children made her think of Lacey. Lacey made her think of Nathan. Nathan made her remember last night, made her remember the kiss.

She couldn't think—or paint—for remembering that kiss.

She set aside that painting and tried another, this one a landscape of the windward beach. It was a wide-angle painting done from a photo she'd snapped when Hugh had taken her up in his seaplane. But her eye was drawn to the rocky promontory where she and Nathan had once stood together, hands clasped, hearts beating as one.

And that brought her to Nathan again. And the kiss.

So she moved on to a landscape of higgledy-piggledy houses perched on the hillside above the harbor. But somehow even the houses reminded her of days long ago when the two of them had walked side by side through the narrow streets, when they'd shared an ice cream, licking madly before it melted in the Bahamian summer sun.

Everywhere she looked, there was Nathan.

Desperate, she got out her sketchbook and tried to figure out other ideas she wanted to develop. She flipped through the photos she'd taken last week, hoping for renewed inspiration. She had shot several rolls of film and had easily half a dozen island scenes that she could work on—children playing in the street; a cricket game on the "cricket grounds" with Daisy the resident horse-and-lawn-mower watching the game; a bunch of happy diners at the Grouper, sitting under palm trees decorated with tiny, colored fairy lights; a shot of two little boys riding the old cannons that had sat on the point, defending the island, for almost 350 years.

They were nothing fancy—just bread-and-butter shots—but they had always captured her imagination before.

Not now.

Now her mind's eye didn't see cricket players or children in the street or little boys swinging their legs on the cannons. It saw Lacey's grin as she'd followed Nathan out the door. It saw Nathan's broad shoulders and strong back. It saw Nathan's back as it had been thirteen years ago, bare and tanned and smooth—

"Argh!" Carin flung the photos aside and raked both hands through her hair.

My God, it was nearly two o'clock and she had nothing—*nothing!*—to show for her day's work. Fiona had asked when Carin brought her the sandwich and Carin had said, "It's coming."

But it wasn't coming. All she could see in her mind was Nathan.

Damn it! Even when he wasn't here, he was here!

Well, fine. If she couldn't be creative, she'd go for a walk. She'd do leg work, make some sketches, get raw material. In the wide-open spaces she'd have other things to distract her.

She put on a pair of sandals, grabbed her sketchbook and her sunglasses and set out.

The air was stifling, steamy and hot, like getting slapped in the face with a hot wet towel—minus the towel. There wasn't a tiny bit of moving air anywhere. The flag hung limp. Even the water in the harbor was flat and still.

Carin headed toward the beach on the far side of the island. If a breeze existed, that's where it would be. The tarmac road burned through the thin soles of her sandals as she walked up the hill. She wasn't outside three minutes before the sweat was running down her back and making damp patches on her shirt.

"You crazy, girl? What you doin' out in the noonday sun?" Carin's neighbor, Miss Saffron, who was eighty if she was a day, looked up from her rocking chair on her shady front porch and shook her head as Carin passed.

"Just out for a little inspiration." She lifted her sketchbook in salute.

Miss Saffron chuckled. "If I be you, crazy girl, I'd be gettin' all the inspiration I need from that man was kissin' you last night."

Her blush came hotter even than the beating sun. Carin wished the tarmac would open and swallow her up. Instead she listened to Miss Saffron's cackling laughter all the way up the road.

She walked past the cemetery and the library, then turned

up Bonefish Road, which led round past the cricket ground, over the hill and through the trees, eventually turning into a path that led through the mangroves down to the beach.

There she found a breeze at last. Tiny waves broke against the shore. To her right there were signs of civilization—a half dozen strategically placed beach umbrellas sat in front of the newly refurbished and gentrified Sand Dollar Inn, an island institution recently turned yuppie since Lachlan McGillivray, Hugh's brother, had added it to his hotel empire.

Carin turned away from it, started to walk, and found no more focus than she'd found trying to paint. The only thing that would help was exertion—making so many demands on her body that she couldn't think of anything at all.

It wasn't smart. She could die of sunstroke. But it was better than spending the rest of the afternoon trying *not* to think of Nathan. So she ran.

She ran. And ran.

She ran until sweat poured down her face. She ran until her breaths came in painful harsh gasps. She ran until she reached the rocks. Two miles. Maybe more. She was exhausted, bent over, gasping for breath. But her mind was clear. She felt calmer, steadier, stronger. Her demon had been exorcized.

Carin shut her eyes and breathed a long, deep cleansing breath. *Yes!*

Then she straightened, turned and began to amble back the way she'd come—and saw, for the first time, the tall dark-haired man and the slender girl in a lime-green cap coming toward her.

Damn!

So much for steadier, stronger and calmer. All Carin's sense of emotional well-being vanished as she realized she'd run right past Nathan's house. Now he would think that she'd come to spy on them!

"Mom! Hi! What're you doing here?" Lacey waved madly, then came running up to her.

"I finished early," she said, struggling to breathe easily.
It wasn't really a lie. She had finished. Just because she
had nothing to show for it, didn't mean she hadn't tried.
"So I thought I'd come for a run."

"In this heat?" One of Nathan's brows lifted.

"I'm quite used to it."

"We finished early, too," Lacey told her. "Dad said
we'd caught enough fish to feed an army and he didn't want
to clean them all. He knows a great fishing spot! Better'n
the one Thomas took me and Lorenzo to!"

"Really?" Now it was Carin's turn to raise a brow. It
didn't seem likely that Nathan would know any such thing,
just having returned to the island yesterday.

Nathan shrugged modestly.

"We're goin' for a swim now," Lacey went on. "An'
then we're gonna cook the fish. Dad says he's good with
a grouper." She grinned. "You can eat with us if you want
to, can't she?" Lacey turned eager eyes on Nathan.

"I wouldn't want to intrude," Carin said quickly, not
looking to see what Nathan's reaction to Lacey's im-
promptu invitation was.

"You wouldn't be," Lacey said.

"You're welcome to eat with us," Nathan seconded.

But Carin didn't want to eat with them. "I'm…having
a guest for dinner," she improvised.

Lacey looked surprised. "Who?"

"Hugh."

She only hoped he was home. If he was, there was no
doubt that Hugh McGillivray, Pelican Cay's "best-looking
bachelor"—his own description—would say yes to pulling
up a chair to her table tonight. Hugh was notorious for
trying to wangle dinner invitations. He also made no secret
of his attraction to her—an attraction that Carin generally
discouraged.

Well, one meal wouldn't get Hugh's hopes up. She just
prayed he wasn't already eating at someone else's house.

"Bring him," Lacey said promptly. "Hugh's just a

friend," she explained to her father. "Remember, I told you about him. He's the one who flew Lorenzo to Nassau."

"Right." Nathan looked at Carin. "Bring him along." There was an edge to his voice. Still Carin hesitated.

"Come, Mom. Please," Lacey begged. "It'd be fun."

It wouldn't be fun at all. But maybe if she brought Hugh, Nathan would think she and Hugh were an item. Maybe he'd realize that he didn't need to stay around Pelican Cay, that Lacey didn't need a full-time father.

"I'll ask Hugh," Carin said. "I'll let you know."

"Seven o'clock," Nathan said. "I can pick you up."

"Hugh has a car. Or we'll walk."

Nathan looked as if he might argue, but Lacey grabbed his hand. "C'mon, Dad. Let's swim. And I want to show you how I can stand on my hands."

Carin swallowed the temptation to tell Lacey not to brag. She should be pleased that daughter and father were forming a relationship, forging bonds, making connections. But she turned away at the sight of Nathan's fingers curling around their daughter's as he allowed himself to be led toward the water. She couldn't look. It made her wish…

She didn't want to wish.

"Dinner?" Hugh looked amazed, then delighted at Carin's invitation. "You're inviting me to dinner?"

A grin cracked his handsome face as he looked up from the boat engine he was working on. Hugh McGillivray had dancing blue eyes and thick dark hair, cheekbones to die for and a once-broken nose that merely added to his appeal. And even with a streak of engine grease on one cheek and another on his bare muscular chest, it was true, what he always claimed—that he was the best-looking bachelor on Pelican Cay.

Or he had been until yesterday, a tiny voice piped up in Carin's brain.

"Yes, dinner," Carin said firmly, ignoring the traitorous voice, not wanting to admit that, even now, in her eyes

Nathan was far more appealing. "Tonight. If you don't have other plans." *Please God, don't let him have other plans.*

"Sounds great," Hugh said cheerfully. "I'll bring the beer."

"Not necessary," Carin said quickly. At Hugh's look of surprise, she shifted from one foot to the other. "It's, um, it's not at my place. Well, it was going to be, but…there's been a change in plans. My, um…that is, Lacey's…father…is on the island…visiting…and he took Lacey fishing and they asked if we'd like to come to dinner." She said all this in sort of a jerky stop-and-go jumble and wasn't surprised when Hugh cocked a brow.

"Invited *us*?" Clearly he was reassessing the invitation and didn't believe her one bit. Carin couldn't blame him.

"Invited me," she clarified. "But I didn't want—I said I was inviting you to dinner—" she flushed a little admitting that "—and Lacey said bring you, and Nathan said yes, do. And, well…you know."

Hugh knew. "Right," he said. "So you want me to go as your boyfriend?"

Carin felt the heat in her cheeks increase. "I don't—I mean, it's not what you think," she said lamely.

Hugh tilted his head. "Oh? And what do I think?"

She put her hands on her hips. "You think I'm still attracted to him. I'm not!"

Hugh's silence told her what he thought of that remark.

"Of course he's attractive," Carin allowed, because it was impossible to deny that Nathan was a damned attractive man. It was the fact that he didn't love her and had left her that she found *un*attractive! "But I'm not attracted to him."

"Uh-huh."

"I'm not!"

"I understand." Hugh nodded solemnly, though there was an unholy light in his eyes. He started to rake a hand through his hair, then looked at the grease on it and wiped

it on his disreputable cutoffs instead. "I get it. You've finally become attracted to me. And about time." His grin
flashed. "Taste comes to Carin Campbell at last."

"Don't you wish?" she teased.

"Don't I," Hugh agreed with just enough seriousness to
make her wonder as she sometimes did, if he was serious
or not.

As long as she'd known him, he'd had one girlfriend
after another. None had been serious. None had lasted. The
only single woman between eighteen and forty she knew
he hadn't dated was her. And not because he hadn't asked.
He had. She hadn't been interested.

"We'll be friends, Hugh," she'd told him. "That will
be better."

"Sez you," he'd complained.

But they'd been friends for four years. Maybe she'd
made a mistake asking him to have dinner tonight. She
didn't want to spoil that by changing things now.

"You're a gorgeous guy, Hugh," she began, "but—"

He held up a hand to stop her. "Don't. If you're asking
me out to dinner, don't start putting qualifications on it."

"No. I just—"

"Don't, Carin," he warned her, a rough edge to his
voice. "What time do we have to be there?"

"Seven. But if you'd rather not—I don't expect—"

"I'm looking forward to it," he said firmly. "I'll be
interested to meet Lacey's father." The speculative look on
his face was further cause for concern. But before Carin
could say anything, he told her, "Right, seven it is, then.
I'll pick you up at quarter to."

"Ok." But as Carin started away from the boat dock,
she still worried. She tended to think of Hugh as her pal,
a carefree, devil-may-care guy, whom every woman on
Pelican Cay lusted after—save her—and who wouldn't be
caught no matter what. Certainly that was the impression
he was always at pains to give.

His reputation, well known among the island's fairer sex,

was that he was a terrific playmate—and bedmate. But in his own words, he'd "never met a woman he didn't like, nor one who made him think in terms of happily ever after."

But Carin also remembered that two years ago he'd taken her flying one afternoon, determined to show off his new toy—the seaplane that he had added to his fleet of charter vehicles. Carin had never taken off or landed on the water before. She'd loved it, had been eager to have him do it again and again.

And while they were soaring through the wild blue yonder getting ready to make yet another approach, and the plane had banked and Carin had taken half a dozen shots out the window, exclaiming all the while how wonderful it was, Hugh had said, "You could do this all the time if you married me."

Carin had laughed. She'd rolled her eyes and said, "Oh, yes. Sure. Right." Because, of course, he wasn't serious. Hugh was never serious in matters of the heart.

He'd laughed, too. He hadn't pursued it. He'd never uttered the word *marriage* again. But every once in a while Carin had caught him looking at her intently, his expression always unreadable.

It had made her wonder more than once if she'd been wrong.

But then immediately she thought, surely not. Hugh McGillivray went through women like she went through tubes of cadmium blue. He was a tease, a charmer and her pal. He could have said no, after all, she told herself. It wasn't as if she was leading him on. He knew she wasn't interested in serious stuff. And neither was he!

"Hey, Carin!"

She slowed and glanced back over her shoulder. Was he going to change his mind?

Hugh was standing beside his disemboweled engine now, looking grubby and sweaty and handsome as sin. And she wished, not for the first time, that she could muster for him a hundredth of what she felt every time she looked at Nathan Wolfe.

"What?"

He grinned. "Wear some sexy little black number with no back, why don't you?"

Lacey had said Carin and Hugh the hunk were "just friends."

It didn't look like that to Nathan.

They weren't exactly holding hands and smooching in public, but when they arrived for dinner they were very definitely a couple. Carin had obviously made an effort to dress up for the occasion. She was wearing a sundress in varying shades of blue. It skimmed her narrow waist and flared at her hips, and it had such thin shoulder straps that it was obvious she wasn't wearing a bra. While the dress wasn't backless by any means, it displayed a lot of smooth, tanned skin, which Nathan watched Hugh the hunk touch as he escorted Carin up the steps.

That annoyed him. It annoyed him further that when she introduced them she called Hugh "my very good friend".

She called Nathan "Lacey's father".

Which he was, of course. But prior to that he had to have been "Carin's lover", hadn't he? He'd been tempted to say so. And he might have if Lacey hadn't been in the room.

Instead he'd got Hugh a beer and Carin a glass of wine and chatted about the fishing expedition he and Lacey had gone on, while he watched the fish he was cooking and tried not to watch Hugh lean back against the deck railing and casually slide an arm behind Carin, obviously staking his claim.

"I think maybe we'll eat out here," Nathan said abruptly. "How about helping me move the table, Hugh?"

"I just set the table, Dad," Lacey moaned.

"It's too nice an evening to eat inside," Nathan said firmly. "Come on." He went in through the sliding doors and was gratified to have made Hugh follow.

After they got the table and chairs moved and Hugh was about to settle back next to Carin again, Nathan suggested she give Lacey a hand. "She made a fruit salad and we've got some garlic bread in the oven that you could bring out."

"I'll help," Hugh said.

"Great." Nathan thrust a platter into his hands. "Hold this for me."

He put Carin at one end of the table, himself at the other and had Hugh and Lacey sit on either side. At least Hugh the hunk wouldn't be able to put his hands on Carin during the meal.

But the connection remained.

When they talked about fishing, Carin said, "Hugh's a great fisherman," and began a story about a time Hugh had taken her and Lacey fishing and they'd had great success because he knew right where to go.

"We didn't do that well," Hugh protested modestly. "Carin thinks less is more because she doesn't like baiting hooks," he told Nathan with a grin.

"I remember," Nathan said tersely. He looked down the table at Carin. "I think I was the first to ever take you fishing, wasn't I?"

Carin paused, a forkful of salad halfway to her mouth. "Were you?" she said. "I don't remember."

Liar, Nathan thought. And he said it with his eyes. He wasn't sure whether he was gratified or not when Carin looked away.

They moved on from fishing to talking about the island economy.

"It's picking up," Hugh said. "Tourist dollars are coming in. They're staying longer, spending more."

"They have more options now," Carin said. "It's not just my place and Miss Saffron's straw shop and the pineapple store and lunch at The Grouper anymore."

Which is pretty much the way it had been—minus Carin's store—when Nathan had been growing up. Pelican

Cay had been a place to come to for complete relaxation, to get away from it all.

"Obviously things have changed," he said gruffly.

Carin nodded. "There are plenty of things to do now. Those who want to can do an afternoon dive or go on a sightseeing boat trip around the island. Three days a week they can take a historical walking tour. The museum is open most afternoons. We've had several historians rave about what a good little collection we've got going."

"An' if they don't want to go to the museum, Hugh will take them up in his plane or sightseeing in the helicopter," Lacey said eagerly.

"And next month we're starting horse carriage tours," Hugh put in.

"So much for peace and quiet," Nathan muttered.

"There are off-islanders who come for two weeks a year and hate the way things have changed," Carin said—meaning him and those like him. "But those of us who have to make a living aren't complaining. We're delighted Hugh and his brother have opened things up."

"It's a matter of balance," Hugh explained. "We're not trying to turn the place into Nassau. We liked Pelican Cay just the way we found it. But we could afford to come and go as we pleased. People who were living here, most of them were barely making it. They needed a few more opportunities."

"And Hugh and Lachlan gave them to us. I got my agent, thanks to Hugh." Carin smiled at him, and Hugh smiled back and winked at her.

Nathan's teeth came together. "Agent?" he said. "What agent?"

"Stacia Coleman. She's a friend of Hugh's. She's in New York."

"I've heard of her." Stacia Coleman was one of the younger up-and-coming agents in the business. His own agent, Gabriela del Castillo, had introduced him to her last fall at a gallery opening in Santa Fe.

"Stacia's sharp," Gaby had told him later. "She has a good eye and good instincts."

Years ago when he'd first seen her work, Nathan had thought Carin had talent. The paintings he'd seen in her shop yesterday had supported that impression. Even so, he was surprised to hear that she was selling her work not just on Pelican Cay, but through Stacia Coleman, as well. Stacia didn't take on friends' friends. She promoted bonafide artists.

"Stacia's arranging a show for Carin next month," Hugh said. There was a note of pride in his voice. "In New York City."

"I'll have to go."

"It's not a big deal," Carin said, just as she had before. She actually looked embarrassed.

"The hell it isn't," Hugh objected. "It's fantastic. You don't get a one-woman show in a New York gallery if you're second rate."

"No, you don't," Nathan said. "Congratulations."

He'd known about her shop. Dominic had mentioned it after he'd visited the cay, months ago. "Arts and crafts stuff. Mobiles, seashells, dust catchers."

"Wonderful pieces," Sierra had countered, giving her husband a playful swat. "You philistine. She has one-of-a-kind pieces. Not touristy shlock at all. Come see the painting I bought."

She'd dragged Nathan into the living room of their Fifth Avenue apartment and pointed to a vibrant, primitive beach scene that complemented the paintings his mother had done even as it outshone them. Whoever had painted it was no amateur.

"Carin painted it," Sierra had informed him.

Nathan had admired it, but he hadn't studied it long. He'd been too blown away by Dominic's other news—that Carin was on Pelican Cay, that she'd been there for the past twelve years, and that she had a daughter called Lacey who looked just like him.

Now he thought about Carin's talent and Carin's promise—and how she'd buried it for all these years in Pelican Cay. Did she regret it? He certainly couldn't tell from her expression.

"So we might get to go to New York!" Lacey said eagerly.

"Not likely," Carin said. "New York isn't exactly my cup of tea."

"But I've never been there," Lacey argued.

Even Hugh argued. "You have to go. It's not every day you get a show like that. Besides, Stacia wants you there."

"I know, but—"

"I'll go with you. Lend moral support," he promised her and reached out to squeeze her hand.

Carin blinked, as if surprised at the offer. But then she smiled. "Maybe."

"Goody!" Lacey cheered.

"Peachy," Nathan growled under his breath.

"I beg your pardon?" Carin looked down the table at him.

He shoved his chair back and said through his teeth, "I said I think I'll bring out some fresh peaches for dessert."

He didn't have any peaches, but he banged around the kitchen until he felt less likely to rip Hugh McGillivray's head off. And then he went back with a couple of fresh pineapples and offered them. "Sorry. Fresh out of peaches. This is all I could find."

"I don't need anything else. It was a lovely dinner. Thank you." Carin sounded like the poster girl for Miss Manners.

"Yeah, it was great," Hugh agreed. "Maybe not as great as whatever Carin would have cooked." He gave her a wink and a grin, then looked back at Nathan. "But it was a pleasure to meet you."

Nathan wasn't going to say it had been a pleasure to meet Hugh. "Glad you could come." That was at least close to the truth. It was, as his father always claimed, smart to size up the competition.

Carin stood up. "We should be going."

Nathan glanced at his watch. "It's not even nine-thirty."

"Some people got up extremely early and had a long exhausting day." Carin glanced at Lacey, who was trying her best to swallow a yawn.

"I'm fine!" Lacey protested when she could open her mouth without her jaw cracking. "I'm not tired!"

"I didn't say you were. It happens that *I* had a very long day." Carin yawned, too.

Nathan wasn't sure if she was faking it or not. Maybe she figured she'd been polite long enough. Maybe now she was desperate to get back to her place, get Lacey to bed, then have mad passionate sex with Hugh McGillivray.

Nathan's jaw clenched so tight that he could feel a muscle pulse in his temple. He drew in a deep lungful of air and let it out jerkily. "Whatever you want."

Carin was still smiling her poster girl smile. "I think we'll just go on, then. Unless you would like us to stay and help clean up the dishes?"

"No."

Wouldn't want you to miss your date for hot sex by helping with the washing up.

His terse reply caused Carin to blink, as if she didn't have a clue what he thought.

Hugh stood up quickly and eased Carin's chair back for her. Then he turned to Lacey. "C'mon, Lace. Time to hit the road."

Like he was her father, Nathan thought, his fingers balling into fists.

Lacey sighed, but she muffled another yawn, which meant, Nathan realized, that she really was tired.

"Get your fishing stuff," Carin directed, "and your backpack and whatever else you brought."

"I'm leaving my photos," Lacey said. "Dad says we'll look at them tomorrow."

"Tomorrow you're helping Miss Gibbs move all those books at the library. Remember?" Carin reminded her.

"Oh, Mom! I don't have to. You know that. It's voluntary. She'll understand."

"No, she won't. She's relying on you. The books need to be moved, Lacey. And you said you'd help. They're refinishing the floor," she told Nathan, "and they need to move all the books to one side. Then next week, they'll move them to the other side. The librarian, Miss Gibbs, asked the kids to help. And Lacey—" she turned her gaze on their daughter now "—volunteered."

"But I—"

"Good for her. I'll help," Nathan said.

Lacey laughed delightedly. "Will you? Oh, cool!"

"Oh, for heaven's sake, Nathan. You don't need—" Carin began.

"The books need to be moved." Nathan quoted her words back to her, arching a brow, daring her to deny what she'd just said.

She clamped her lips together.

Getting no denial, he shrugged. "So I'll help. Do me good to volunteer, too. Since the island is going to be my home now...." He stared hard at Carin, making his point, then for good measure turned his gaze on Hugh, as well.

He was gratified to see the other man's obvious surprise.

"Then Lacey can come back here with me after," Nathan went on smoothly, "and we can go over her photos. We didn't have time today. Give you a chance to do your painting," he said to Carin. "And Lacey needs to help me on my book, too."

Her mouth opened as if she were going to argue. Then she shrugged those nearly bare shoulders. "I'm sure Miss Gibbs will be delighted to have your assistance. And that's nice that you and Lacey can work on your book. But I won't be painting. I'll be working in the shop. I only paint on Wednesdays." She stepped through the open sliding door into the house, heading straight for the front door, then turning once more to say politely, ''Thank you again for the lovely meal. Say thank you, Lacey,'' she instructed their daughter.

''Thanks, Dad.'' Lacey flashed him a grin that, thank God, didn't look forced.

He reached out and gave her ponytail a tug. ''Anytime, kid.''

Hugh stepped around Nathan and opened the door for Carin, then turned back and offered Nathan a grin and a handshake. ''Hope we meet again soon.'' Pause. ''Carin and I will have to have you for a meal.''

It was a blatantly territorial comment and Nathan knew it. He shook Hugh's hand, pistols at dawn not being an option. But nothing required that he respond to that ridiculous remark, so he didn't.

''Night, Dad.'' Lacey said brightly, turning to grin up at him. ''It was a great day, wasn't it?''

''Yeah, great,'' Nathan echoed hollowly. He managed a smile. Just. And one last tug of her ponytail.

For her he was glad that it had been. For him, seeing Carin walk away with Hugh's hand pressed possessively at her back, the blessings had been decidedly mixed.

CHAPTER FIVE

ELAINE, Lorenzo's seventeen-year-old sister, hurried into the shop at ten minutes past nine. "I'm sorry! I'm sorry! I'm sorry I'm late!"

Carin, who was dusting, blinked. "Late? For what?"

"Nathan said to be here at nine."

"*What?* Nathan said *what*?"

"To be here at nine. That you needed me to work every day." Elaine looked delighted. "I'm so glad. I was so sick of waitressin'. My feet hurt sooooo bad."

Carin stared at her. "When did you see Nathan?"

"Saw him yesterday afternoon. Him an' Lacey came by to talk to my dad after they went fishing. Oh, you mean about workin'? Didn't see him. He called last night. Said you had a big show in New York an' you needed more time to paint. I was that happy, I can tell you!"

"Ah." Carin hesitated. "Um."

"What you want me to do? Want me to dust? If your cash register is like The Grouper's I won't have any problems with that." Elaine was so eager that Carin couldn't simply say, There's been a mistake. Go home.

But there had definitely been a mistake! And Nathan Wolfe had made it! How dared he?

"Just...yes, here." Carin thrust the duster in Elaine's hand. "I need to make a phone call. I'll be right back."

There was a phone by the register, but Carin went to the one in the back room. She punched out the number of Nathan's cell phone, which he'd given her yesterday. She'd been sure she would never need it. She was wrong.

"What do you think you're doing?" she demanded when he answered.

"Ah, Elaine arrived."

"Yes, damn it, she arrived! And you're just going to have to get down here and tell her you've made a mistake and she has to go home. And you'd better hope she hasn't given notice at The Grouper!"

"I gave it for her. Stopped in this morning when Lacey and I were on our way to the library."

"What!" Carin was outraged. "You had no right!"

"Elaine asked me to. And you need time to paint. You said so," he reminded her.

"That doesn't mean you're supposed to hire someone to work for me! I can't afford—"

"I'm paying her."

"No!"

"Well, she's not going to work for nothing."

"You're not hiring my help! You presumptuous bastard! You—"

"Stop shouting in my ear. Ms. Gibbs can probably hear you all the way across the room. This is a library, you know."

"I don't want—"

"You don't want me here. That's the bottom line. Too bad. I'm staying. And I'm trying to make life a little easier for you."

"Then leave," Carin muttered.

"Look, Carin, I know you don't think much of me. So be it. You never gave me a chance. You shut me out. Well, now I'm back. And like it or not, you're stuck with me."

"That doesn't mean—"

"It means I'm taking an interest in Lacey's life. Lacey's life involves you. You've got a terrific opportunity here. I'm trying to give you a chance to benefit from it. I'll keep Lacey during the days so you won't have to worry about her. Elaine will take care of the shop. And you can paint."

Carin's jaw tightened. He was so reasonable. He was so right, damn it! "You can't pay her."

"We'll discuss it later. Go paint."

"I—"

But there was just dead air. He'd hung up.

Damn it! Carin fumed, she paced, she fussed. She didn't want to be beholden to Nathan Wolfe. She didn't want him running her life.

But it was true, what he'd said—this gallery show was a once-in-a-lifetime opportunity—and Stacia did want more paintings. In fact, she'd called this morning to see how Carin was coming on them.

"Good," Carin had said, which was only a small lie. "Moving right along."

"Wonderful. Glad to hear it. When will you be finished?"

"I'm not sure yet. Can I call you in a week or so?"

"A week?" Stacia sounded worried. "I'm going to be out of the city for a few days. How about I call you when I get back? I'll need to come down so we can pack them up for shipping."

Ordinarily Stacia wouldn't be bothered doing any such thing. It was outside the realm of her job. But she was sure Carin had enormous sales potential.

"You're a phenom ready to be discovered," was what she'd said. And she was pulling out all the stops to make sure it happened—even going so far as to say she would come to the island herself and make sure that the paintings were packed and shipped properly since there was no "pack and ship" on Pelican Cay.

Stacia had a lot invested in her in terms of time and effort and expense. Of course, she stood to get plenty in return if Carin was the success Stacia thought she would be.

But that meant Carin had to come through with enough work to make mounting the show worthwhile. And that meant she should have hired an Elaine weeks ago, but she hadn't had the money to do so.

Now Nathan was taking Lacey and offering to pay Elaine.

"I can pay him back," Carin said aloud now.

"You talkin' to me?" Elaine called from the front of the shop.

Carin took a breath. "No. I was talking to Nathan." She would pay him back. And he wouldn't be able to stop her. "Here," she said to Elaine. "Let me show you the ropes."

Elaine learned things quickly. By ten Carin felt she could leave her on her own in the shop, giving her the admonition to call if she needed anything.

Elaine shook her head. "Nathan said not to bother you."

Carin narrowed her gaze on the young woman. "Call me," she said. "Or I'll fire you."

Elaine flashed a broad grin. "Well, when you put it like that…"

Carin went home. Zeno, hoping for a snack, tagged along after her. She gave him a bit of ham and left him sitting on the porch. Then, somewhere between fierce and furious, she headed for the studio to tackle her work.

Lacey couldn't have been happier.

As the days passed and she went fishing with her father or shot photos with her father or just walked on the beach and talked to her father, she couldn't have had a better summer.

Carin couldn't have been more of a wreck. Of course she was happy that Lacey was forming bonds with her father. But for herself, as she heard daily the tales of Nathan and Lacey fishing, helping move books at the library, taking photos in the cemetery or going swimming or snorkeling, Carin felt bereft.

She felt hollow. Lonely.

And she couldn't help thinking about what it would have been like if they could have done these things together as a family—the three of them.

That was stupid, of course. If they had been a family, Nathan would never have been able to do what he'd done. He wouldn't have been able to pursue his dreams, find his path, focus on his goals. He would have grown to resent her—and their child.

Too, if she'd announced she was pregnant with his child, she would have caused a huge rift between him and Dominic. Lacey talked a lot about her dad and his brothers when they were growing up. She loved to recount the "Nathan and Dominic and Rhys stories" that her father told her. It was clear they loved and respected each other. And there was no way Carin would have wanted to come between them.

So it was just as well she'd kept her mouth shut. Just as well she'd accepted her fate—and there was no sense in bemoaning the fact that they had no memories together.

But you could have now, some niggling little inner voice kept telling her. *You could have said yes when Nathan asked you to marry him.*

But she was selfish. She didn't want Nathan marrying her out of duty. In her heart she was still a romantic. She wanted to marry for love.

She was thinking about this when Hugh stopped by on Friday after work. He stuck his head in the studio and asked, "How's it going?"

And Carin said wearily, "It isn't," because thinking about Nathan had depressed her and she hadn't been able to paint much for the last half hour. She decided to take a ten-minute break and have a cup of tea before sending Hugh on his way.

Now he was leaning against the kitchen counter with a bottle of beer in his hand. watching her sympathetically as she paced and muttered. "I don't know how I'm going to get this done."

"You're trying too hard. You need to relax. Come out to dinner with me."

"I can't. I've got to work. But every time I try I start to think. And then I stop working. I don't know what to do!"

"Kiss me."

"What?" She stared at him as if he'd lost his mind.

"Kiss me," Hugh said. "Now." He set the beer on the counter, took two steps across the room and hauled her into his arms.

Carin was so amazed she let him. She wrapped her arms around him to keep her balance, and was the recipient of a deep hungry kiss.

"Hard at work, I see," a voice drawled from the front porch. "Don't let me interrupt."

Carin froze at the sound. But Hugh took his time finishing the kiss before he drew back and looked over Carin's shoulder at Nathan.

"Not a problem. We can continue later," he said smugly. "Looking for Lacey?"

"As a matter of fact, I'm not. I'm looking for her mother. I came to see if you—" he looked pointedly at Carin and not at Hugh "—wanted to join us for dinner, seeing as how you've been working so hard all day." Scorn positively dripped. "Figured I'd give you a ride over. Lacey thought it might save you a little time if you didn't have to cook. Give you more time to paint." His gaze narrowed and his tone became even more scathing. "But I see you've got other, more important things to do."

Carin flushed guiltily and was annoyed that she was re-acting at all. It wasn't his business what she was doing! Or with whom.

"Hugh stopped by after work and I took a few minutes' break," she began.

"You don't owe me any explanations."

"You're damned right I don't!"

"So don't waste your breath. Are you coming with me for dinner or are you going to be too busy going to bed with lover boy?"

"Now there's a thought." Hugh grinned.

Carin glared at him, then at Nathan. "I'm going to paint, damn it. So you can both just get out of here now."

Hugh sighed. "Ah, well, I can wait," he said easily, then bent his head and dropped a light kiss on her lips. He winked as he sauntered out the door past Nathan and down the steps. "See you later, sweetheart."

Nathan didn't budge. "So, *sweetheart,* are you coming or not?"

"Not," Carin said. "I need to work."

Nathan regarded her through narrowed eyes. "You'd better work," he said. "You'd better be painting your sweet little heart out."

As Carin watched, he turned on his heel and stomped down the steps. At the bottom of the steps he turned and looked back up at her. "I'll have Lacey home at nine. So whatever you and lover boy get up to in the meantime, you be sure to be painting by then. Fair warning."

As he drove away, Carin stuck her tongue out at him.

Dominic called to see how it was going.

"It's not," Nathan said testily.

Rhys called to offer advice.

"It's not the same as with you and Mariah," Nathan said with all the patience he could muster. "Mariah *told* you when she was pregnant. She *wanted* you to be part of Lizzie and Stephen's life."

Obviously, his brothers talked to their father. Next thing Nathan knew the old man was on the phone.

"What do you want?" Nathan growled.

"Nothing," Douglas said airily. "Just called to shoot the breeze."

"Uh-huh." And pigs could fly. "And you're not going to ask about my love life?"

"Don't have to, do I?" Douglas said. "I think it's pretty clear from your tone that you don't have one."

Nathan ground his teeth.

"Sure you don't want me to come down and lend a hand?"

"Yes, damn it, I'm sure. And no, damn it, I don't!"

"Giving you a hard time, is she?" Douglas said, sounding almost sympathetic.

"I don't want to talk about it."

He knew what he was doing. He hoped. Besides, for the moment progress on the Carin front was at a standstill. There was nothing to talk about. She was painting—or so she said. And he was spending the days with Lacey.

He and Carin talked stiltedly when he picked Lacey up or dropped her off. Occasionally Hugh was there when Nathan brought her home.

"Helping you paint, is he?" Nathan found himself snarling more than once.

She didn't answer. It was hard to pick a fight with someone who ignored your provocation. And she did seem pretty paint-spattered much of the time, so he didn't have much of a leg to stand on.

Still, having to leave Lacey there with her mother and Hugh didn't make for restful evenings.

Actually, it made Nathan nuts. He took to going to The Grouper after he dropped Lacey off. There was sure as hell no point in going back to his place. All he'd do there would be to pace the floor and mutter things about Hugh McGillivray's maternal ancestry. Knocking back a beer or two or three with the locals was a much better idea.

At least, though his relationship with Carin was nonexistent, he and Lacey were getting on like a house afire.

He spent most days with Lacey. The day after the dinner at his house, they'd helped Miss Gibbs move library books. Then they'd gone back to his place and had begun to look at slides and talk photography. They did that now almost every day. She was smart as a whip and she had a good sense of composition. When he explained something, she asked questions, and she got the point.

Every day he spent with her, he learned more about her—and her mother—and felt twin twinges of anger and sadness that he hadn't had a part in her life until now. He blamed Carin. Sometimes he wanted to throttle Carin.

But if he was honest, he understood why she hadn't told him.

He'd been so focused in those days. He knew he was going to be a photographer, knew in his gut he could do it. But he also knew how much it would demand of him, how hard the work would be, how single-minded he'd have to be.

Fighting his father's determination that he go into the family business had been nothing compared to the obstacles he'd had to overcome to get where he was. He hadn't needed more obstacles.

Carin had known that.

It wasn't easy looking in the mirror when he thought about how self-absorbed he'd been.

He wasn't self-absorbed now. He wasn't single-minded. Gaby, his agent, was calling him every few days making offers and suggesting ideas—all of which would mean traveling—and every time, Nathan said no.

"I'm staying put," he told Gaby.

He was enjoying his time with Lacey. He was opening up the world to her. And she was opening up a particular small slice of it for him.

She was an eager student. She always wanted to take photos. Every day, no matter what else they did, they spent time doing that. At first he just let her take photos that interested her. But after a few days of that, he suggested she start looking for specific things. Patterns, themes, specific subject matter.

They shot trees, they shot flowers, they shot buildings

and birds and kids and fishermen. They shot old men at work and playing dominoes under the shade trees.

Sometimes they picked a topic—heat, water, happiness, symmetry—and spent the day shooting whatever they saw that expressed it.

In the evenings they developed the black-and-white film together. They took the slides to Deveril's, which had an overnight developing facility, then spent the next morning comparing the differences and similarities in the way they viewed things.

It was as instructive for Nathan as he hoped it was for Lacey.

He was fascinated to discover what interested her, to learn more about the way she looked at the world. And she rose to every challenge he offered, focusing on it, thinking about it, trying to see what she could bring to it that would be something he hadn't thought of. Sometimes she wanted it too much, tried too hard.

"Don't push it," he advised her. "It's about vision and about potential, but it's mostly about patience. You've just got to be there. The opportunity will come."

It was true in photography. Great photos came to those who were prepared, who knew what they were doing and were prepared to wait.

And as the days went by and nothing seemed to happen, he hoped to God it was true in life—in his life—with Carin.

His theory, which was not at all the theory subscribed to by his father or even by Dominic, for that matter, was that showing up and sticking around were half the battle.

"It's all about opportunity," he told himself, just as he'd told Lacey about photography.

But as one week went by and then another, he didn't see any opportunities.

Lacey did her best to try to throw them together. It was no secret their daughter wanted them together, even though she never said so outright.

"Don't push," Nathan advised her when she was trying to get her mother to come to dinner with them one night. "It doesn't do any good. She might show up because you asked her to, but it won't be because she wants to."

"I know, but—"

"And she'll go home irritated and more resistant than ever."

"Maybe, but—"

"So we'll just cool it," Nathan counseled. And tried to take his own advice.

But as the days passed, it got harder and harder to simply bide his time.

As the days passed Carin thought Nathan would get bored, get fed up, get antsy, be ready to leave.

Instead he stuck around.

Not only did he stick around, but he and Lacey bonded completely. They fished and swam and wandered all over the island, according to what her glowing daughter told her every evening. He listened to her and talked to her. He took her seriously. As far as Lacey was concerned, she could not have a better father.

"I wish he'd been here before," she said more than once.

"He wishes he had been here before, too."

Carin tried to take that with equanimity. "Really? Did he say so?"

"No. 'Cause he's too polite. But I know he feels that way. I can just tell."

Which, of course, made Carin the bad guy of the piece. Good old Nathan wasn't even complaining because she'd done him out of twelve years of their daughter's life. Perversely it made her angry.

It was hard, too, because she felt such conflict. She didn't want to feel beholden to Nathan, and yet she was. He was saving her bacon by taking Lacey every day, by having hired Elaine, by allowing her to paint.

Even so, it was hard to feel grateful. She didn't *want* to feel grateful. And yet she knew she owed him.

More guilt.

And then there was Hugh. Carin was grateful to him, too. He made a point of stopping around in the evening along about the time Nathan would be bringing home Lacey. He stood in her kitchen, beer bottle in hand, acting like he'd been there all evening, giving her intimate little smiles and winks designed to make Nathan believe she and Hugh were an item.

He kissed her, too. And she let him—in front of Nathan. She told him they were friends. He said of course they were friends. But then he winked at her. And he kissed her. And there was something in the way he looked at her.

Even more guilt.

Oh, God, what a mess everything was!

The painting, wretchedly slow as it was, was the most successful part of her life! At least when Stacia had called on the weekend, she'd been able to say, without lying, that she had two paintings finished and the others were coming along.

"Terrific!" Stacia had been delighted. "I'm so glad. Do you want me to get you reservations for a place to stay?"

"No. Thanks. I still don't think we'll be able to make it." Every spare penny she had was being put away to reimburse Nathan for Elaine's salary.

"But you could use a holiday," Stacia argued.

"That wouldn't be a holiday," Carin said truthfully. The very notion of going to her own opening scared her spitless. "A holiday is where you have a good time."

Stacia laughed. "Keep painting. Let me know when you're getting close to finished and I'll be down."

"Will do."

No, she wouldn't go to New York. But maybe they could take a vacation to another of the islands. Stay a week or two before school started.

And when they got back, with luck Nathan would be gone.

Surely he had to leave sometime. He couldn't just stay on the island forever. A man who made his living traveling to the four corners of the earth wasn't going to be able to do that on an island five miles long and half a mile wide. The subject matter just wasn't here.

"Once you've seen one lizard, you've seen them all." Carin smiled to herself.

Maybe she could ask when he dropped Lacey off tonight. Since Hugh wasn't here—he'd flown a charter to Nassau and would be returning tomorrow sometime—it would be good to have another distraction. Something to annoy Nathan.

Since he got annoyed every time she brought up the possibility that he might not spend the rest of his life on Pelican Cay, that would be a good one.

But shortly before nine, when she heard the car pull up out in front, the engine kept on idling even as the car door shut. Half a minute later, Lacey banged into the house and the car drove away.

"No Nathan?"

"Dad's got company. Her name is Gaby."

"Gaby?" What kind of name was that? It called to mind blonde bimbos with big boobs.

"His agent," Lacey said.

"Oh." The blonde bimbo disappeared as fast as she'd come. "Well, that's nice," Carin said briskly. Nathan's agent arriving had to be a good sign. "When did she arrive?"

"This afternoon. We had dinner with her."

"And is she here to get your father to go back to work?" Carin asked, hoping she didn't sound as eager as she was.

"He is working," Lacey said, offended. "He works every day on his book."

"I mean in the field. She must want him to go and take more photos."

Lacey hunched her shoulders. "Dunno. They didn't talk about that. You don't think he'll leave, do you?"

"I don't know." Clearly Lacey wanted him to stick around. Carin didn't want to get in the middle of an argument about it.

"He's got a lot to do on his new book," Lacey said. "The one he's picking out photos for. And she was talking about him doing a show at her gallery this winter."

"Gaby has a gallery?"

"Uh-huh. In Santa Fe. It has a Spanish name." Lacey scrunched up her forehead, thinking. "Something about sombreros?"

"Sombra? Sombra y Sol?" Even Carin had heard of Sombra y Sol. It was one of the best-known galleries in Santa Fe.

"Yeah, that's it. Sombra y Sol."

"I thought it belonged to Gabriela del Castillo."

"Yeah." Lacey bobbed her head. "Gaby."

That was Nathan's Gaby? Though Carin had never met Gabriela del Castillo—having lived in a Caribbean backwater for a dozen years, that was a given—she'd certainly heard of her.

Gabriela del Castillo was a force to be reckoned with.

The widow of famous art patron, agent and entrepreneur, Enrique Castillo, she took over his gallery and his business after his death a few years back. At first, gossips said she was coasting on her late husband's coattails. But it hadn't taken Sra del Castillo long to dispel that notion. She had an eye for talent—and she was a terrific marketer.

Gabriela del Castillo was highly respected in the art world now. Sombra y Sol displayed some of the finest photographers in the world as well as some of the most successful artists in other media. It was one of the galleries Stacia had mentioned when she'd told Carin that if her show in New York was a success they might be able to take her work elsewhere. Carin had privately thought Stacia was aiming a little high.

It didn't surprise her that Gabriela del Castillo was Nathan's agent. It did surprise her that Sra del Castillo was humoring him about his staying on Pelican Cay. But maybe she would crack her whip after she'd been here a couple of days. Carin envisioned her as an elderly, ramrod-straight Spanish matron with snapping black eyes and an astute business mind.

"He showed her my photos," Lacey said. "She liked them. She says I'm a chip off the old block. Maybe she'll show my photos someday."

"Maybe," Carin said. "How long is she staying?"

"Dunno. They were going to The Grouper. He said he was going to take her out for a little local color."

Carin grinned. "Well, I hope she enjoys it."

It was hard to imagine a seventyish widow enjoying the steel band at The Grouper, but maybe Nathan was trying to broaden her horizons a little. "Is she staying at the Mirabelle?"

The Sand Dollar was a hip, yuppie spot on Pelican Cay while the quietly elegant Mirabelle, tucked away by a cove at the south end of the island, was the poshest small inn on the island. It was one of several that Hugh's brother, Lachlan, had bought in the past year. The Mirabelle was where all the VIPs stayed when they came to Pelican Cay.

Lacey shook her head. "She's staying at Dad's."

Carin was surprised to hear that. But then, maybe Sra del Castillo was a family friend. Perhaps she and her husband had been friends of Nathan's father. Douglas had to be about seventy now. And from what Carin remembered of him, he had his finger in many pies. She wouldn't be surprised if Sombra y Sol was one of them.

"Well, I'm sure she'll find it comfortable and quiet," she said. "She must be tired if she just arrived today."

Lacey shrugged. "I guess."

Carin yawned. "I'm tired, too. Time for bed. What time is your father picking you up tomorrow?" she asked as she shut off the light in the kitchen and shooed Zeno out onto the front porch.

"He's not," Lacey said as she climbed the stairs. "I'm going fishing with Lorenzo and Thomas."

Carin stopped, one hand on the newel post. "What? Since when?"

Lacey looked back at her. "Dad called Thomas and asked. He and Gaby have work to do. They said I'd be bored. And Thomas said it was okay."

"And he didn't think to check with me?"

Lacey lifted her shoulders. "He said he didn't want to bother you, on account of your painting and all."

"So he imposed on Thomas?"

Lacey looked offended. "Thomas is glad I'm coming. He says I'm a 'civilizing influence' on Lorenzo." She turned again and went up the steps.

Carin, following, shook her head. "I wonder. Well, I guess...if Thomas agreed. But I still think your father should have discussed it with me."

"He says you never want to talk to him."

It was true, of course, but galling that he had mentioned it to Lacey.

Still she went off to bed, heartened and blessing Gabriela del Castillo for her arrival. It wouldn't be long now and Nathan would be gone. Carin felt better than she'd felt since Nathan had appeared back on Pelican Cay.

The morning went well. The painting went well.

Knowing that Lacey was with Thomas and Lorenzo and not with Nathan somehow freed up a little of her creativity. Knowing that Gabriela del Castillo was at this very moment most likely leaning on Nathan to get back to work freed up some more.

Carin actually got some work done after Lacey left in the morning.

It was the first time in a long long while that she'd been able to focus, to think, to feel as if she were "in a zone" as far as her work went. She even whistled while she worked, contemplating the departure of Nathan as she did so.

She would have worked straight on through the afternoon, but Elaine expected her to bring lunch. She had done it every day, using it as an excuse to check on things, to see how Elaine was doing, to answer any questions the young woman might have.

Ordinarily, too, it was a nice break because she was getting so little done that being allowed out of the studio for twenty minutes or so was a treat.

Today she grumbled as she assembled Elaine's lunch and bundled it into the basket of her bicycle. It wasn't far to the shop, only a few blocks. But it was quicker to ride Lacey's bike there and back, and today—for once—Carin was actually in a hurry.

She pedaled off toward the shop, focusing on the new painting that was taking form in her mind. She didn't see Miss Saffron's cat dash across the road.

She didn't see Zeno race after him—not until he was right in front of her. She slammed on the brakes, jerked the handlebars and swerved just in time to see Nathan, his hand on the small of the back of an absolutely gorgeous blonde woman, going into the grocery store.

Carin, gaping, wobbled wildly, swerved madly and hit a pothole.

The bike flipped. So did the lunch.

So did Carin.

And then she went splat.

CHAPTER SIX

"*CARIN*! Good God, Carin! Are you all right?"

Asinine question. Of course she wasn't all right!

She'd flipped right over the handlebars of the bike! If he shut his eyes Nathan could see it still, in slow motion, Carin sailing through the air, arms flailing in an attempt to get her balance—and lay now in a crumpled heap in the road.

"Go inside. Tell 'em to call the doc." He didn't look to see if Gaby followed his directions or not. He had already hurdled the stair railing and was sprinting down the street toward Carin.

She was conscious. She was moving. She was scraped. He saw blood and he could hear her swearing a blue streak, saying words that would have shocked him if he hadn't been tempted to say them himself.

"Don't move," he instructed as he crouched beside her. "Damn it, Carin! Stay still!" he commanded when she struggled to get up.

"Bloody, bloody—! Oh, hell! Owwww!" She was scrabbling on the ground, trying to pick herself up, but one arm wasn't cooperating. And Nathan was afraid to touch her for fear of making things worse.

She had an abrasion on her cheek. Her legs were scraped, her hands bloody. And her arm—oh, God—her arm!

"Stop moving, damn it!" Nathan snapped at her. "You've broken your arm."

Carin looked at him, stricken, white as a ghost. Only her lips and lashes had any color. "I haven't! Oh damn! Oh hell! Oh—" She swore desperately. "I can't have broken my arm!"

"You have. Stop moving."

"You're not a doctor! What do you know?"

"I know you aren't supposed to have an elbow halfway down your forearm."

She jerked her gaze down and really looked at it for the first time. Then she looked back at Nathan, went even whiter, and her eyes started to roll back in her head.

"Damn it, Carin! Don't faint!" He did his best to get her head down, trying to avoid her arm, easing his around her, feeling her whole body tremble. He had no doubt that she was in shock. "It'll be okay. Gaby's got 'em calling for the doc."

"Gaby," she mumbled and shook her head as if she was dazed.

"My agent," he explained. "That's her name." It seemed stupid to be talking about Gaby now. He wanted to see how badly Carin was hurt.

But people began appearing to stand around—Lyle from the grocery store, Emmalyn from the bakery, Otis who ran the hardware store. And Miss Saffron, holding her damned cat. Zeno was there, too, looking worried.

"Is she all right?"

"Carin, you ok?"

"Oh, Carin!" It was Elaine. "You're hurt! You're not dyin'?"

Carin saw her and dredged up the faintest of smiles. "Not dying," she affirmed. "Your, um, lunch." She managed a weak wave of her hand on the unbroken arm toward the contents of the bag that had been in the basket of the bike.

"Forget the lunch." She stopped at the sight of Carin's arm. "Your arm! It's your *right* arm!"

The significance of this seemed to hit Carin at the same time it hit Elaine—and Nathan. Her right arm.

"I can't paint!" There was panic in Carin's tone now. "Oh, my God, I—"

"Here's the doc," Nathan broke in as Maurice pulled up in his Jeep and Doc Rasmussen climbed out.

He ran quick, practiced hands over her and turned to Maurice. "Call Hugh. Tell him we need to get her to Nassau." As he spoke he put a temporary splint on Carin's arm.

"Hugh's already in Nassau," she said weakly.

"We'll get him back here," Nathan promised. "Call McGillivray and tell him to get his ass home."

Maurice shook his head. "Be lots faster if Molly takes her."

"Who's Molly?"

"Hugh's sister," Carin answered. "Yes, Molly can do it."

Nathan noticed she wasn't arguing about having to go to the hospital. But he wasn't sure about Hugh McGillivray's sister. He'd met Molly McGillivray one day when he'd needed some work done on his boat's motor.

Lacey had said she knew who could fix it—and had taken him to see a girl she'd introduced as Hugh's sister.

Nathan had hardly believed it. Hugh had dark hair and blue eyes and was, even Nathan had to admit, pretty damned good-looking. The girl he'd met had carrot-red hair, freckles enough for a dozen Irishmen, and looked like a seventeen-year-old boy! She'd been wearing cutoff jeans, a baseball cap, and a T-shirt advertising a bar. With a smear of grease on her cheek and a wrench in her hand, she looked like a poster child for Tomboys R Us.

She'd fixed his engine in no time flat.

Now he said, "How many sisters does McGillivray have?"

"Just Molly."

Nathan had been afraid of that.

But Doc Rasmussen nodded. "Let's get her in the car. Call Molly and tell her we're coming. Maurice, you can drive us."

Nathan would have objected, but Carin, of course, was already trying to rise on her own, with Doc doing his best to support her.

Nathan stepped in. "Here," he said and scooped Carin into his arms before she could protest. "Open the door, Maurice."

Carin was still trembling as, slowly and carefully, Nathan carried her to the car and eased her into the front seat. He felt a shudder run through her before he got her settled. "You okay?"

She nodded shakily. Her head fell back against the headrest and she closed her eyes for a brief second before opening them again and meeting his gaze. "Yes. Thank you."

"No thanks necessary," Nathan said gruffly. "Doc can ride with you. I'll take my own car."

"You don't need to come," Carin said quickly. "You need to be here. For Lacey. She's out fishing with Lorenzo and Thomas. Of course you know that. You set it up." She sounded aggrieved.

Nathan wasn't going to get into that with her now. "I'll see you at McGillivray's."

"Lacey—"

"Lacey will be fine."

She woke up in the hospital.

At least she supposed she was at the hospital.

She felt dazed and fuzzy-minded and her mouth tasted terrible. She looked around. She was in a private room, which didn't seem right. There was no way she could afford a private room. Even dazed and confused, she knew that.

She moved her gaze slowly—it was almost the only thing she could move—trying to take it all in.

Her arm was in plaster halfway to her elbow. There were ominous metal screws sticking out of the plaster. One leg was raised on pillows. Her hands were bandaged. Her lips felt cracked. There was something stuck to her cheek.

Every muscle in her body hurt. Even when she blinked, she could feel it.

"Look who's awake."

Her head jerked around and she almost screamed at the pull of the muscles. And very nearly screamed again at the sight of Nathan, unshaven and bleary-eyed, standing over her.

"Wha-what are you doing here?" Even her throat hurt. Probably because they'd stuck some tube down it while they had her knocked out.

"Watching you."

"Well, don't." If there was ever a time she didn't need him around it was now. She knew she sounded petulant and probably even childish. "Just let me alone."

"Thought you might like to know how Lacey is."

Her gaze snapped back to him. She started to sit up. "What's wrong with Lacey?"

"Nothing's wrong with Lacey," he said quickly, his tone soothing. "You were worried when we left, so I thought I'd stay around and let you know she was fine. I figured you'd want to know."

"Yes. Of course. Thank you. Where is she?"

"At Maurice and Estelle's. Hugh will bring her by later." His jaw tightened briefly. "We ran into him at the airfield and he insisted on coming to the hospital with us. When you were out of surgery, he flew home. He'll tell Lacey."

"And he's bringing her?"

"Later today. And he'll take her home again."

Knowing that Lacey was all right eased Carin's mind. That didn't help, though, when it came to her arm. She looked at the cast with the pins, and then at her leg. "What did they do to me?"

"Rasmussen called in an orthopedic surgeon, who set your arm. He put a couple of pins in it, said it would heal faster that way. Your ankle is sprained. X-rays came back negative for breaks on that," Nathan reported. "You've got some abrasions. Lots of grit in your skin. They picked that out while you were unconscious." He nodded at her face and at her gauze-wrapped hands. "It should heal up pretty fast. Doc said a couple of months and you'd be good as new."

"A couple of months?" Carin tried not to wail the words. "My show…"

"Don't worry about your show."

"Easy for you to say," she muttered.

"Ah, good. You're awake, dearie." A nurse appeared in the doorway, a bright white smile on her ebony face. "How you be feeling, then?"

"Just ducky," Carin muttered. But it was actually nice to see someone other than Nathan.

"Pain medication wearing off?" The nurse shook a pill out into a tiny paper cup and gave it to Carin. "You just take this. You feel better soon." She held a glass of water so Carin could sip it and get the pill down. "You get lots of sleep now an' you heal right up," she went on. "Don't worry 'bout a thing. Your husband, he take care of things for you."

The water went right up Carin's nose. She coughed and snorted and gasped and every muscle in her body screamed.

"Oh, dear. Oh, dear. You drink too fast. Go slow. You got to go slow, dearie," the nurse said, completely misunderstanding the reason for Carin's coughing fit. The nurse put the glass out of reach and waited until Carin had stopped choking. "There now. You go slow."

"He. Is. Not. My. Husband." Carin wheezed out the words. She shot Nathan a fulminating glare.

The nurse looked surprised, then as her gaze turned to Nathan, she looked accusing.

In return Nathan looked both implacable and inscrutable. Whatever he had told the doctors and the hospital staff, it had apparently involved him being a close relative.

Now he shrugged, as if to say, Want to make something of it?

Clearly the nurse didn't. "You want more water now you stopped choking?" she asked Carin.

"No. Thank you," Carin added after a moment, banishing the rude child. She gave the nurse a wan smile and was rewarded with a pat on the hand.

"Don't you fret now," she said. "Whatever he is, he cares about you." Then, giving Nathan a smile, too, she headed for the door. "You need anything, you push that button," she pointed to the one by Carin's hand. And then she was gone.

And the two of them were alone again.

"Go away," Carin said after a moment.

Nathan didn't bother to answer. He didn't bother to move, either. He just sprawled in the chair by her bedside, looking tired. His dark hair was ruffled and uncombed, as if he'd run his hands through it. Dark stubble shadowed his cheeks and jaw. He was wearing a rumpled long-sleeved blue shirt and a pair of jeans faded at the knees to almost white. They were what he'd been wearing when she'd seen him right before she'd gone sailing over the handlebars of her bike.

"What time is it?" she asked wearily, when it was clear he wasn't going anywhere. There was some light coming through the window, but not much. It looked to be getting dark.

Nathan glanced at his watch. "Just past seven."

"I've been out six hours?"

"Eighteen. It's seven in the morning."

She stared at him. "Seven in the morning. Tomorrow? I mean, I've been here since yesterday?"

Nathan nodded. "Yep."

"And you've been here…"

"Since we brought you in."

No wonder he looked as if he'd been run over by a truck.

And Carin didn't even want to think what she must look like. "You should go home," she said.

"I will." But he still made no effort to move.

"Don't you have a hotel room?"

"Didn't need one. They let me stay here."

All night? He'd sat beside her bed all night? Carin was mortified and felt oddly teary at the same time.

"Well, you didn't need to," she told him.

"I promised Lacey I would."

And what could she say to that? Her fingers curled around a handful of sheet, and she shook her head, overwhelmed, exhausted, hurting even though the pain killer was beginning to take effect. It made her feel woozy. Her eyes shut.

"Go to sleep," she heard Nathan say. His voice seemed to come from far away. "Get that rest the nurse was talking about."

She strove to open her eyes. "You—" But of their own accord her lids closed again. "You should go..."

The last thing she heard was Nathan say, "Don't worry about me."

Nathan was doing enough worrying for both of them.

Whatever "opportunity" he'd been waiting for, he'd never imagined this one. The sight of Carin flying over those handlebars was one he would take to his grave. And the vision of her chalk-white face and the way her eyes went all glassy from shock still had the effect of a punch in the gut every time he called them to mind.

He hadn't left her side except for the time she'd spent in the operating room. Then he'd paced the hallway cursing and muttering, calling himself seven dozen kinds of a fool for being so damn "patient" so damn long.

He should have just hauled her off to a justice of the peace as soon as he'd arrived. It was what his father and Dominic would have done.

It was fine to let people go their own way if they didn't matter to you. But Carin mattered!

He loved her.

The moment he realized it was frozen forever in time as if he'd framed a shot, clicked the shutter and captured the mind-boggling amazement that came with it.

He had told himself he'd come for Lacey. He had a daughter; he wanted to know her. And Carin? He hadn't let himself think about Carin.

When he couldn't help but think about her, he'd focused on his anger at her not telling him, on his pain that she hadn't loved him enough to trust him to do the right thing. And after he'd got here and faced further rejection, he'd done his best to get his heart to reject her, too.

But it wouldn't. Because his heart knew what his head had tried to deny—that he had come because of Carin. Lacey had been a part of it, the catalyst, but not the deepest reason.

That had been Carin all along.

He'd had a lot of time to think about it during the fifteen hours or so, after his epiphany. He had sat by her in the recovery room. He'd walked alongside the gurney when they'd taken her back to her room. He'd scarcely left her side since. He'd answered questions from the doctors and nurses. He'd fielded visitors—and she'd had several, including Hugh, who had run into his sister at the airfield.

Hugh had come up to the room right after she'd returned from recovery and had insisted on seeing her. "Lacey will want to know how she is," he'd said.

"Getting along," Nathan had replied. But he knew that Hugh was right, that Lacey would expect a report and that it would be better for her if she knew Hugh had actually seen her mother. So he let Hugh in.

"For a few minutes." He'd stayed right by her side, and he'd made sure Hugh understood that he was in charge.

Hugh hadn't seemed inclined to dispute it. There were

no grins and intimate glances. He kept a respectful distance from Carin's sleeping form, standing at the foot of the bed, looking pale and worried and shaken, but uninclined to fight Nathan for the place of responsibility.

On the contrary, after he'd looked at Carin, he'd turned his gaze toward Nathan and said, "You're staying?" he asked as if he already knew the answer.

"Yes."

"I'll bring Lacey tomorrow."

Nathan had wanted to say that it wasn't necessary. But of course Hugh's offer was sensible and was what Carin would want. So he'd agreed. "That'd be good."

Hugh nodded and looked back at Carin, then sighed. "What a mess." Then noting how Nathan had stiffened, he grinned faintly. "Not Carin."

"Definitely not Carin."

"She's going to be crazy when she realizes she won't get enough paintings finished."

"I'll take care of it."

As soon as Hugh left, Nathan had used the phone in the room to call Gaby. He'd told her to call Carin's agent to tell her what happened, to see what could be done. And then he'd gone back to sitting beside Carin.

He wished he could at least hold her hand. But both hands had been bandaged and she was asleep and there was nothing he could do at all.

Only sit there and know that he loved her.

He wouldn't go away.

They were going to keep her in the hospital three days. Three!

It was ridiculous, Carin told the nurses, the doctors, everyone who came to see her. Everyone knew they were sending people home from the hospital the moment they'd pinned them back together these days.

"Not here," said Dr. Bagley, who had done the surgery.

"Not my patients. You stay until I say you are ready. You cooperate, maybe you go home tomorrow."

And since there was no way she could go without help, Carin stayed—and cooperated.

But she didn't need Nathan bloody Wolfe staying with her!

She told him that. She told the nurses and doctors and everyone else who came to see her, too. Often. Hourly sometimes.

No one paid any attention. Not even Hugh. He came bringing Lacey the afternoon after she'd had surgery, and she'd tried to get him to take Nathan home with him. "He doesn't need to be here," she'd said. "I don't want him here."

But Hugh only shrugged and said not very helpfully, "He says he's staying."

Something had happened between Nathan and Hugh while she'd been asleep. There was no convincing Nathan that Hugh meant anything to her anymore. It didn't take a genius to figure that out.

So she tried to enlist the aid of the nurses. "Tell him to go away," she said to each of them in turn. "He's invading my privacy."

"Ah, dearie, you know you'd miss him," said one.

"Send that great hunk of handsome away? Not on your life, ducks," said another.

"Only if I can take him home with me," said the youngest, batting her lashes and slanting hungry grins Nathan's way.

"Don't be daft," the senior nurse said to Carin. "Without him you'd be in a ward, not in a private room. I'd give my arm for a man who cared that much for me. Hasn't left you once."

"You need a change of clothes and a shower," Carin told Nathan.

"I took a shower," Nathan said, nodding toward the

bathroom attached to her room. "And Gaby brought me a change of clothes just this morning."

"Good for her," Carin said sourly.

Nathan just grinned at her. "See? Clean jeans. Fresh shirt. Brought me my shaving kit, too. I'll shave when you take a nap."

Carin could see, now, that he had cleaned up. And though he obviously still looked tired, his stubbled jaw only made him look rakish and more handsome than ever. She felt like an ugly witch by comparison.

"Gaby's looking forward to meeting you."

"What!"

"She'll be along in a little while. She couldn't stop this morning. Had a business meeting this morning. But when they get things sorted out, she'll be along to see you."

"She doesn't need to stop and see me," Carin said hastily. "What does she want to meet me for?"

"Because I've told her all about you," Nathan said.

Whatever that meant. Carin didn't even want to think. She didn't have time in any event because moments later the door to her room opened and the beautiful blonde Carin recognized as Gaby came in.

She wasn't alone, either. There was another woman with her. She came running toward Carin, long, dark hair flying.

"Oh, my God, Carin! You poor thing! I didn't believe it when Gaby told me!"

Carin gaped. "*Stacia?* How did you—" Nathan's agent had told hers that she was in the hospital? Oh, dear God. "I was going to call you," she began, trying to sound calm and in control to Stacia, all the while shooting Nathan a furious glare. "I've got...got two of the paintings done. I know that's not—"

"Not to worry," Stacia said, patting her unplastered arm. "You need to rest. To get well. You need to take care of your arm. Even your hands are bandaged." She was tsking, making horrified sounds.

"I'll be all right," Carin said. Dr. Bagley hadn't told her she wouldn't be. He'd said she might need some therapy but she could do that. "I just can't get all six of the paintings done now, though."

If Stacia dumped her, Stacia dumped her. This show had been going to be her "big break," and she might never get another. But there was no crying over what had happened. It had happened—and she simply had to go on from there.

"No problem," Stacia said, giving an airy wave of her hand.

Carin blinked. "No…problem?"

That wasn't what Stacia had been saying the last time they'd talked. "You think you've got enough to make the show go on?"

"Of course," Stacia said emphatically. "It's all sorted out. It will be wonderful." She beamed at Carin, then at Nathan. "Having such a wonderful photographer's work as a complement to your paintings will bring patrons out in droves."

"*What!*" Carin tried to sit bolt upright, but gasped at the pain and sank back against the pillows to stare aghast at Stacia. "What are you talking about?"

"Nathan's offer. You know we needed more," Stacia said, perfectly matter-of-factly. "I told you that. I told you six more large pieces minimum. Better ten. Or lots of smaller ones. So you finished two more. And Nathan offered his work to fill in the gaps. Island shots, right?" She looked at Nathan for confirmation.

He looked a little uneasy, as well he might. If looks could kill, Carin thought, he'd have been worse off than she was.

"I don't need Nathan bailing me out," she said to Stacia.

Stacia blinked, then said, "Oh, but you do. We don't have enough otherwise."

"Then we won't do it!"

Stacia just looked at her. For a full minute she didn't say a thing, just looked, and let Carin realize how stupid and petulant and childish she sounded. It didn't even take thirty seconds. Irritably she did her best to shrug.

"I don't like to be beholden," she said irritably. "I wanted to do it on my own."

"But circumstances don't permit. And you will," Stacia assured her. "In time, you will. But for now, this is perfect. It will showcase your work in the company of a man who shares a vision with you. Different media, same subject. Wonderful. And I hear that your daughter has done some fine work as well."

"Lacey?" Carin looked from Stacia to Nathan to Gaby.

Gaby was nodding. "She's very talented. We thought we might feature all three of you." She beamed. "A family affair. Island Eyes."

While Carin listened, stupefied, they chatted on, as if it were really going to happen. They talked about logistics and shipping and framing and all the practicalities that meant they were serious. They discussed Lacey's work as if they were familiar with it. They mentioned different pieces. They talked about balancing her work and Nathan's with Carin's paintings.

Every once in a while they consulted Nathan. But they talked as if Carin weren't even in the room. When the nurse appeared, she took one look at Carin's pained expression and misunderstood the situation completely.

"Out," she said to Gaby and Stacia. "You're tiring my patient."

They didn't seem to mind. "We can finish this over lunch," Gaby said cheerfully. "No sense in bothering Carin about it."

"Of course not." Stacia came over and patted Carin's hand. "Don't you worry about a thing. Gaby and Nathan and I will take care of everything."

"We certainly will," Gaby seconded. "It was lovely to meet you at last, though I'd have preferred other circumstances," she added. "And don't worry. Everything will be fine. We'll see to it."

Carin looked from one woman to the other, and finally at Nathan. "No reassurances from you?" she asked sarcastically.

He shrugged, but met her gaze steadily. "Trust me," he suggested.

She didn't.

Not an inch.

How could she when he just bullied his way in and took over her life?

First he insisted on staying with her the whole time she was in the hospital. Then he arranged for his agent and hers to get together and come up with this ridiculous combined show, this "family affair," which everyone else seemed to think was wonderful and which Carin knew was a sham.

They weren't a family, damn it!

But when she pointed that out to Nathan, he said, "We could be."

And she knew that was his way of saying he was still willing to marry her. Obviously the Wolfe notion of duty ran very very deep.

She found out just how deep when she finally got out of the hospital and Hugh flew her home to Pelican Cay.

Of course it was too much to hope that Nathan wouldn't be with her every step of the way. Even when she had Hugh right there to help her, Nathan insisted on carrying her across the tarmac and helping her into the helicopter.

"Where's Lacey?" she demanded. Lacey had flown over with Hugh once, but she'd been so stricken by the sight of her mother all banged up that Carin had told Hugh not to bring her again until she was ready to come home.

Lacey needed to feel that her mother could cope. And seeing her in the hospital, barely able to do anything for herself, didn't lend itself to the notion of coping. After three days she was better. She could feed herself. She could hob-ble around—just. She had thought Lacey would be here to witness her progress and her return home.

But Nathan just said, ''She's getting the house ready for you.''

And Carin had to be satisfied with that. In fact, it was probably just as well Lacey hadn't come, since the mere trip to the helicopter wore Carin out.

She tried to appreciate the beauty of the island as Hugh took off and eagerly pointed things out to her. But the com-bination of fatigue and pain medication got to her before they'd gone far, and she felt her eyes close.

When she woke up, she found her head against a warm male chest. She jerked and looked up and found herself staring into Nathan's blue eyes.

''You okay?'' he asked.

She pulled away and tried to sit up. ''Fine. I'm fine.''

She managed to stay awake until Hugh set the copter down on the small landing field near the cricket grounds. Then he carried her bags to his waiting van and Nathan carried her.

''I can walk,'' Carin protested.

But Nathan ignored her. ''Humor me,'' he said. ''I love carrying wriggling females.''

She shot him a look of annoyance and stayed perfectly still to spite him, then realized that was exactly what he had in mind.

He tucked her into the second seat of the van and clam-bered into the back one, then reached up and slung the door shut. ''All set,'' he told Hugh who was in the driver's seat.

Hugh put the van in gear, and they rumbled out of the field and onto the road. Carin was leaning forward eagerly now, looking forward to seeing the town, to seeing her house, to being home again. It felt as if she'd been gone a year, not merely a few days.

"Hugh! My house is that way!" She pointed to the right fork when Hugh took the left.

Hugh just kept driving, bouncing them along the rutted road toward the far end of the island.

The penny dropped. "Oh, no." Carin protested. "You're not taking me to Nathan's!"

"You can't stay at your place," he said practically.

"Certainly I can! Stop this car! Hugh, turn around!"

But Hugh neither stopped nor turned. He wound through the jungly woods heading directly for Nathan's place.

"Damn it!" Carin shoved herself up, making her arm hurt. "You can't kidnap me like this!"

"Fine. We'll just go back to the copter and take you back to the hospital."

"Take me home!"

"Can't." He shook his head. "Doc said you need care."

"I'll get care. Lacey can—"

"Lacey's a child," Nathan said firmly. "And you are an adult. So why don't you try acting like one."

Carin glared at him, furious at being told off that way. "How dare you! She's my daughter! She can—"

"No doubt she can," Nathan cut in. "*Our* daughter is bright and capable and she would probably bend over backward to do whatever you wanted her to do because you're her mother and she realizes how much you've done for her. But—" he fixed her with a hard level stare "—I would hope you're not selfish enough to ask her to do it."

Carin opened her mouth, then closed it again. She sat, rigid, glaring at him, hating him for putting her at such a disadvantage, for being right, for making her feel like a fool. She didn't speak, just glowered.

He didn't back down. "She's at my place now, fixing up a room for you, making it nice for you. She and Estelle have been working on turning my dad's office into a bedroom for you so you can be on the main floor and you won't have to climb stairs, which you would have to do at your house…''

"I could have," Carin said sulkily.

"And the very least you can do," Nathan went on, "is to be grateful to her for her efforts. You can stop acting like a spoiled child and start acting like a mother."

Carin felt as if steam was going to come right out of her ears. "I'm *not* selfish! You're the one who's being selfish! Pushing into our lives, taking over, shoving into my gallery opening, forcing me to stay at your place—''

"Get it out of your system now," Nathan said implacably. "Because you'd better not carry on like this in front of Lacey. Bad enough you're doing it in front of Hugh."

Hugh? Dear God, she'd forgotten about Hugh, driving silently on toward Nathan's, listening and not responding at all.

"Whose side are you on?" she asked him now.

His gaze flicked up, and their eyes met in the rearview mirror. He looked abashed and apologetic. "Nath's just trying to help, Carrie."

Carin arched a brow. "Nath?" she echoed. "Are you two buddies now?" She looked at Hugh accusingly.

"We've, um, talked…''

"Talked? And what did he tell you? Did he tell you he's trying to run my life?"

"And you're making it such a pleasure," Nathan said dryly.

Carin flushed and glared at him.

"The doc said you couldn't be going up and down stairs and you had to have someone with you or he wouldn't let you leave. You know I don't have any place to put you up. And Lachlan's place is full this time of year. And it would be a hell of an imposition on Estelle and Maurice.''

"I know that," Carin muttered.

"So Nathan said you could stay with him."

"Out of the kindness of his heart," Carin grumbled, disbelieving.

"Exactly," Nathan said, his tone gruff but something of a smile lurking at the corners of his mouth. Their gazes met. Something electric seemed to sizzle between them.

If she were healthy and whole she would run a mile, Carin thought.

"You're doing this for Lacey," she told Nathan sternly. *Not for me.* "Right, Nathan?"

He just looked at her. "What do you think?"

CHAPTER SEVEN

SHE WAS IN TROUBLE being at Nathan's 24/7.

But she was stuck and she knew it.

As the doctor had predicted, she couldn't manage on her own. It wasn't just climbing the stairs in her house with her badly sprained ankle that she couldn't have done. She couldn't do simple things like cooking a meal or washing dishes. She certainly couldn't frame her pictures or work at the store.

Just getting through the day was a struggle.

"Accidents do that," Nathan said, taking her weakness in stride and with far more equanimity than she did.

Of course he did, she told herself, because he was getting what he wanted!

But why any sane man would want to be stuck with a cranky, annoying invalid and an exuberant twelve-year-old girl she couldn't imagine.

Nathan seemed to take her crankiness and Lacey's endless enthusiasm in stride, too.

He pretty much ignored the first and he actually encouraged the second. Mostly he seemed to be able to cope.

She wanted to be furious with him, to hate his bossiness and his presumptuousness and his general all-around taking over of her life.

But it was hard to hate the man who carried her to the bathroom, when she needed to get there, because she couldn't use crutches and her leg wouldn't let her put weight on it at first. It was hard to dislike him when he cooked her dinner and brought her breakfast and fixed her lunch. And it was hard to stay angry with a man who got up in the middle of the night to check on her and who every night bedded down on the sofa in the living room so he would be close enough for her to call if she needed something.

She wanted to turn away from him, to fight him, to resist him and, damn him, he was making it almighty difficult.

Of course, from the start she'd been cornered into calling a truce. After what he'd said about Lacey worrying about her, she'd had no choice. And once they got there, she'd understood what he meant.

Lacey had been standing on the porch, practically bouncing with joy at the sight of her mother. She had been so eager to have Carin back home, so obviously worried about her, and so delighted that they would all be there together at Nathan's and that "everything would be all right now," that Carin knew she had to try to make sure it was.

That meant she couldn't fight with Nathan when Lacey was around. But the fact was, as the days went by, she couldn't seem to fight with him, anyway.

He was still bossy and interfering and thought he knew best. But he was also making their daughter feel happy and secure. He was allowing Lacey to be a child instead of her mother's caretaker.

Carin was grateful for that.

At the same time, though, it made her want more. It made her want things she'd wanted years ago, when she'd been starry-eyed and in love.

And she didn't want to want that. Loving Nathan and not being loved in return simply hurt too much.

Still, at the moment she couldn't change things. She had to stay here until she was well enough to go home. When at last she and Lacey were on their own again, she would do what she could to restore the distance between herself and Nathan.

In the meantime…in the meantime she was living dangerously.

Oh, yes.

Every day she felt herself sucked further into the web of desire. It was, in some ways, like the week they'd spent together all those years ago. She hadn't wanted to want him then, either. But what her mind knew, her body disagreed with, and her heart…her heart was torn.

Watching Nathan day after day—studying him surreptitiously when he was cooking dinner in the kitchen or out on the deck repairing a railing or at the desk in the living room, bent over his light table picking over his slides—was a treat and a torture at the same time.

She'd always liked looking at Nathan. And his lean, agile young man's body had matured well. He was still lean, though not slender. His shoulders were broader than she remembered, his arms were harder and more muscular. There was a bit more hair on his tanned chest.

Nathan's chest, Carin decided—purely from an artist's perspective, of course—was a work of art. She knew that some men worked hard at the gym to achieve masculine perfection.

Nathan's beauty was a by-product of working hard. And wherever he moved—whether around the kitchen or the garden, on the beach or in the water—he did so with an effortless masculine grace.

He had always been a man who was comfortable with his body.

And it was all too easy to remember what he'd been like in bed.

Carin knew she shouldn't think about that. But it was impossible not to.

She was a captive of her injuries, stuck in the house where they'd slept together with far too much time on her hands. It was too easy to look at him and remember. The days were hot, the nights were barely less so. She saw a lot of Nathan's bare, tanned skin.

She touched it, too. At night when he came to check on her, he was usually bare-chested and wearing only a pair of shorts. Before she could walk and he carried her into the bathroom or out onto the deck, she felt those strong hard arms supporting her. Her body was pressed against the firm warm wall of his chest.

She remembered when he'd been hot with passion, remembered when their bodies had linked, when their hearts had beat together, when, however briefly, the two of them had become one.

They weren't restful thoughts.

She tried to stay out of his way.

"You don't have to stop and fix lunch for me," she'd protested when he'd brought her a sandwich and a cup of soup the day after she arrived. It was enough that he had cooked dinner for them the night before and had brought her breakfast in the morning.

"I'm fixing lunch for me," he'd said patiently. "Easy enough to make two sandwiches."

She would have looked foolish if she had made an issue out of it. So she'd thanked him politely and had eaten the lunch—which had been very good—and every day after that he brought lunch to her in her room or carried her out onto the deck on nice afternoons so she could enjoy the weather.

Bad. Worse, instead of disappearing again, he sat and ate with her.

She couldn't tell him not to. It was his deck.

Nor could she refuse to answer the perfectly polite questions he asked her and take part in the perfectly pleasant conversations he began. So they talked. Carefully at first, as if they were treading in a minefield, which in many respects they were.

At first Lacey had hovered around every minute, obviously afraid that leaving them alone together might be a disaster. But as the days passed and the truce endured, like any twelve-year-old, she got bored with spending every minute with her parents. She went to Lorenzo's. She went to Marcus's. She went to the shop and helped Elaine or she went to see Hugh and Molly. In other words, she resumed her regular life.

She had already gone and they were eating lunch one afternoon when Nathan asked Carin about her painting.

"I remember thinking you had talent when I saw the stuff you showed me," he said. "But you didn't have a 'style' of your own then."

"You're right. But then I met Gretl."

And she told him about Gretl Hagar, the internationally known Austrian folk artist who had spent a winter on Pelican Cay when Lacey was small.

"Miss Saffron owned the shop then. And I was working for her," Carin told him, "and dabbling in various artsy things when I could. Gretl used to come by the shop and play with Lacey and talk to me about her work. She encouraged me to find what I liked to do. I told her I didn't have a lot of time to do anything, except when Lacey was napping. And she said to come to her place and she would play with Lacey a couple of mornings a week and I could work."

Nathan's brows lifted. "Gretl Hagar played with Lacey?" Obviously, even he knew who Gretl was.

Carin nodded, smiling as she remembered that winter. Gretl had been so kind, so supportive.

"She said it was important to mentor. Someone had helped her get started. She helped me. I've tried to do that, too. Though I'm not nearly the caliber of artist Gretl is."

"You're very good," Nathan said flatly.

"What about you?" she asked. "Did you have a mentor?"

He thought a minute. "Mateo," he said. "Mateo Villarreal."

"I remember Mateo Villarreal."

He looked surprised. "You do?"

"Well, I remember your mentioning him. You'd been

climbing with him before you...before you came here for the wedding.''

And just like that, the years seemed to fall away. The ''Do Not Touch'' and ''Do Not Mention'' signs vanished and the past came rushing back.

When she'd first met Nathan he'd just come back from an Andean expedition with Chilean mountain climber Mateo Villarreal, a man so well-known that even a non-climber like Carin had heard of him.

During the week they'd spent together, Nathan had told her plenty of Mateo stories. Mateo, he'd assured her, made a guy like Dominic look easy-going. Mateo was intense, focused, demanding and absolutely reliable. Also very funny. It had been easier to think of Dominic as a ''whole person'' and not just a scary one when she'd heard Nathan's stories about Mateo.

She hadn't gone through with the wedding, though, because in telling the stories, Nathan had endeared himself to her even more. One Mateo story she remembered particularly well because it had, in a way, made her reevaluate her own situation.

In those days, Nathan had said, he hadn't been much of a climber. He'd had to push himself to keep up with Mateo on even a moderate climb. Of course, the climb itself wasn't what he'd gone for. Nathan had been after photos. He'd told her there was a particular route he'd wanted to climb and Mateo had said no, he wasn't ready.

Nathan had argued. ''A man needs to test himself.''

But Mateo had been adamant. ''There's testing and there's foolishness. And it's crucial to know which is which. It's fine to stretch. But you need to respect your limits.''

It was respecting her limits that had made Carin jilt Dominic. In the abstract, the notion of being married to Dominic Wolfe had been thrilling. He was gorgeous, wealthy, strong, capable, responsible—everything a woman could want in a man.

He was like Everest. Both towering and tempting.

Not a challenge in which a novice could succeed. And the closer she'd come to their wedding day, the clearer that had become.

During the week before the wedding, Nathan had attempted to show her the softer side of Dominic—the human side, the gentle side. He'd shown her that Dominic had traits that made him human, that she could relate to.

It wasn't Dominic she'd doubted in the end.

It was herself.

Facing marriage to Dominic, Carin had learned her limits.

Now she wondered if she was pushing the limits again—sitting here talking to Nathan, feasting her eyes on him, enjoying his company.

She finished her glass of iced tea. "I'd better let you get back to work," she said abruptly. Nathan looked startled. A flicker of something—annoyance? irritation?—crossed his face. But then it was a mask of politeness again.

He stood up. "I'll take the dishes into the kitchen. Do you want to stay here or would you like me to carry you back to your room?"

Carin shook her head and stood up carefully. "I'll walk."

She didn't need him touching her. Didn't need more memories or more temptation. It had been a week since her accident. It was time she did what she could for herself. She took a halting step.

Nathan's jaw tightened as he watched. "Carin." His tone was warning.

She shook her head. "I'm fine," she said fiercely. "Go take the dishes into the kitchen."

He didn't move, just stood there, prepared to catch her if she fell.

She wouldn't fall!

She saw a muscle ticking in his temple as she made her way past him and slowly limped into her room.

Enough.

Nathan wanted to tell Carin he'd had enough. Wanted to step in right now and tell her how it was going to be—that she was going to let him carry her across the damn room, that they were going to talk about what had happened between them all those years ago, logically and rationally for once. Then they were going to put it behind them, marry each other, turn the three of them into a family, and that was going to be that.

A hundred times since her accident he opened his mouth to say those things. And every time he'd back away again.

His father could have done it. Dominic could have done it. Hell, even Rhys probably could have done it!

Nathan couldn't.

He wanted to marry her. No question about that. If he'd come back out of duty first and a healthy curiosity about the one woman he'd fallen hard for in his whole life, that wasn't why he was here now. He was here because he loved Carin Campbell.

But he couldn't ask her to marry him now because, damn it to hell, when he married her, he wanted her to love him, too!

She didn't. Not anymore.

Once she probably had. He understood now—with maturity and the experience that came with years of casual dating—that while other girls might hop into the sack with a man just for the fun of it, Carin had never been one of them.

When she'd made love with him that night, she'd been doing exactly that—making love.

And he understood now what he hadn't understood then—that he'd loved her, too—in his way.

But he hadn't been in any position to do anything about it then. In fact, what had happened between them that night had scared him to death.

It wasn't only betraying his brother's trust that had been wrong. It was that he'd become involved with Carin. He'd told himself he was merely entertaining her while she waited for Dominic. He'd charmed her and teased her and talked to her—and found himself drawn ever deeper by his attraction to her.

He'd wanted her. And he'd had her with no thought as to what the consequences might be.

He'd overstepped his limits.

It went back to exactly what Mateo had been telling him when they'd gone climbing. There were some things that were, for the time being, out of his reach.

"You're not ready for that peak," Mateo had told him.

He hadn't been ready for Carin, either.

And as soon as he'd made love with her, he'd known it was wrong. He'd felt gut-punched. Queasy. Desperate. Guilty. Every bad thing he could imagine.

If he'd never fully understood the Sunday school story about forbidden fruit, he'd had firsthand experience of it when he'd made love to Carin.

He couldn't undo what he'd done. And heaven help him, he had still wanted her—as wrong as it was. So he'd done the only thing he knew how to do at the time.

He'd run.

He'd gone as far and as fast as he possibly could. He'd turned his back on all of them, consumed with guilt, with knowing he'd overstepped. If he couldn't undo it, still he'd tried desperately, with the naiveté of youth, to put things back as best he could.

It couldn't be done.

The world had changed.

Carin had changed. At the time, of course, Nathan hadn't had any idea how much. Now he knew that by taking her love when he'd had no right to it—when it should have been beyond his reach—he had completely altered her life.

He hadn't realized then that he'd also altered his own.

Now he did. And he was still trying to put things right, knowing even as he did so that the odds were against him. He'd had his chance with Carin all those years ago. He'd blown it. He had no right to expect her to look kindly on his efforts now.

Still he couldn't stop trying. Couldn't walk away. He'd promised Lacey he wouldn't. But this was about more than Lacey. It was about Carin and him. It was about second chances and trying again.

He was smarter now. Older. More mature. He had something to offer her—if he could only get her to see it.

Sometimes—like at lunchtime—he thought he was making a bit of progress. Sometimes she was like the old Carin, eager and interested, easy to talk to. Sometimes they could have a genial conversation.

And then, all at once, she would pull back, the way she had this afternoon. One minute they'd been talking comfortably about Mateo Villarreal, and the next minute the wall between them had slammed back down again. He was on one side, she was on the other, and she wouldn't even let him touch her.

He'd enjoyed the conversation. He'd been looking forward to touching her. Having the excuse to carry Carin from one place to another was a pleasure—and a pain.

It was wonderful to have her in his arms, to touch her soft skin and rest his chin against her silky blonde hair. He lived for those moments, for being close enough to breathe in the scent of her, to surreptitiously rub his nose against her hair, to accidentally on purpose brush his cheek against its softness, to rub the pad of his thumb along her arm, to let his fingers slide down the backs of her bare legs.

He prowled the house, irritable and unsettled, needing to work on his book, unable to focus on it at all.

Talk to me he wanted to demand.

But he didn't think he wanted to hear anything she might have to say.

And nothing he could say apparently made the slightest difference to her.

He had to show her. Had to prove that he had changed. Had to convince her by his actions.

But first he needed a cold shower.

The door creaking open startled him.

It wouldn't have awakened him had he been asleep. Of course he wasn't. He'd barely slept, it seemed, since Carin had come to stay. At first he'd deliberately stayed awake to hear her if she needed him to help her, to carry her.

But she didn't need him now. Not like that.

But he stayed awake anyway. Couldn't help it. It was too easy to lie in bed and remember lying there with her. Too easy to think about her creamy smooth flesh because he'd been touching it lately.

And all the cold showers in the world didn't help if the minute you had one, you started once more thinking about the woman who had made you need the shower. So Nathan was awake and restless when the door creaked open and soft limping footsteps came down the hallway.

He stopped breathing. But his heart still thundered so loudly that he wondered if she could hear it.

Was she coming to him?

That had been one of the cold-shower fantasies—that one night she would find her way from her bed to his. Now, hearing her footsteps, Nathan wanted to sit up, to reach out to her. His aroused body ached for her.

The footsteps slowed, then paused at the archway into the living room. He swallowed. He could see her silhouetted in the moonlight as she looked toward him.

Should he move? Shouldn't he?

Still she stood there, one hand braced on the doorjamb. Nathan took a slow, careful even breath.

Come to me. As she'd come to him all those years ago.

He shifted, made a sound, wanted her to know he was awake.

She jerked and stepped back from the doorway.

"Carin?" He couldn't *not* speak. His voice was ragged. "You okay? You, um, warm enough?"

On that long-ago day she'd been cold after the storm and he'd warmed her. God, he wanted to warm her again, wanted to take her into his arms and—

"I'm fine," she said quickly, her voice sounding raspy. "I...I was just on my way to the bathroom. Sort of using the wall for balance. Sorry if I bothered you." And she hobbled quickly away.

He stayed where he was, cursed his foolishness. Maybe he shouldn't have said anything, maybe she would have come closer, maybe...

The water ran in the bathroom, then the door opened and she limped back, quickly this time, and went straight past the archway to the living room. She didn't pause or look his way.

The door to her room shut with a decided click.

Nathan let out a harsh breath. He flung himself over onto his side. Hell! He tried to put her out of his mind; he tried to forget.

He needed another cold shower, but he'd be damned if he would advertise his distress. He glanced at his watch, sighed, shifted against the sheets, turned and finally hauled himself up off the sofa.

His body was taut with arousal. He stared toward Carin's room, willing her to open her door again, willing her to stand there in her shift in the moonlight, willing her to want him the way he wanted her.

But the door stayed shut.

And finally there was no help for it. Nathan eased open

the sliding door, grabbed a towel off the railing and went swiftly down the steps, headed toward the beach.

The cool night air did little to assuage his hunger, the colder ocean water into which he flung himself helped only a bit.

He got through the night. But first thing in the morning he took himself off early to spend the morning working on a new project, a sort of architectural history of the island's houses. It was a far cry from the work he usually did, but he was enjoying it—or he would have been if he hadn't wanted to enjoy something else—making love to Carin!—more.

If he were smart he would stay away all day, but as lunchtime approached he picked up some conch fritters from Perry at the fish shop and headed home. With a salad and a cold beer, they'd be an unexpected treat. He knew Carin liked them as much as he did and he was looking forward to seeing her grin of delight.

"Hey," he called as he bounded in the door. "Guess what I've got!"

She wasn't in the kitchen, so he headed for the deck. Most days lately she had been setting the table for the two of them out there. But the table was bare and she wasn't on the deck, either.

"Carin?" He went back in and headed for her room. "Carin? Are you okay?"

The door was ajar. He pushed it open—and stood stock-still and stared.

The bed had been stripped, the quilt haphazardly folded at the bottom. The desktop was bare. The closet doors were open. Her clothes were gone.

"What the—!" Nathan whirled around and sprinted out of the room and up the stairs to Lacey's room.

It was just as bare.

"Carin!" It was a bellow now.

He banged Lacey's closet doors open, kicked the corner of the bedstead, cursed and charged back downstairs.

And then he spotted it—on the kitchen counter. A note. A *note,* for God's sake! A *thank-you* note!

"'Dear Nathan,'" he read through clenched teeth. "'I want you to know how much I've appreciated your hospitality. It has been a great help. I'm doing so much better that I don't want to impose any further, so Lacey and I are going home. We really appreciate…'" Blah, blah, blah.

He crumpled the note. Slammed his fist on the counter! Flung the bag of conch fritters clear across the room!

Then he jumped in his car, whipped it around and drove straight back to town. He slammed on the brakes in front of her place, practically knocked Zeno over as he pushed through the gate, took the steps two at a time and banged open the door without even knocking.

Carin was sitting on the sofa eating a piece of toast. She looked startled, then resolute, then damned guilty.

"What are you doing?" she demanded.

"*Me*? What am I doing? You're the one who picked up and stole out without a word to anyone! Just what the hell do you think *you're* doing?"

"Eating lunch," she said deliberately misunderstanding. "Would you like some?"

"Damn it, no, I wouldn't like some! I brought you lunch at home! Conch fritters! Come on, we're going back."

"No, we're not. I'm not. We imposed on you long enough. I'm fine now."

"Oh, yes, I can see how fine you are." Her arm was still in the cast and in the sling. She was still wearing a T-shirt—his T-shirt!—because she couldn't fasten buttons well.

"I need to get by on my own. It was time."

"So you snuck out," he accused her.

Her lips tightened into a firm line. "I did not sneak out!

I just didn't want to argue. You told me we shouldn't argue in front of Lacey," she reminded him.

"How do you know we would have argued?" He was prowling around her living room. It was barely big enough to swing a cat in. He nearly tripped over the rocking chair as he swung around and glowered at her.

"Educated guess," Carin said dryly. "If I'd said I wanted to go home today, would you have said, oh sure, I'll drive you right over?"

Nathan scowled and scuffed his toes on the braid rug. "I would have tried to make you see reason. That's *not* arguing."

"Right. If *I* do it, it's arguing. If you do it, it's making me see reason." Carin shrugged equably. "I didn't want to see reason," she said reasonably. "So I called Maurice and asked him to come get me."

"Just like last time," Nathan said bitterly.

Carin stiffened. "It is not at all like last time. I wasn't running away today. I was coming home. Besides, you and I were not getting married."

Nathan stared at her in stony silence. He felt betrayed, as if she'd pulled the rug right out from under him.

"Why?" he demanded. "Was it so hard living with me?"

She hesitated. "You were very kind. I—"

"Kind!" He spat the word. "I didn't do it to be kind, damn it!"

"I know that," Carin said, an edge to her voice.

"Then—"

The front gate banged. "Here comes Lacey. We are not arguing in front of Lacey."

Nathan opened his mouth.

"Your rule," she reminded him.

Nathan swallowed a retort as Lacey burst through the door. "Hi, Dad! How come we're back here, Mom?" She gave Nathan a brilliant grin, which faded a bit as she looked at her mother.

Good, Nathan thought. Let her explain.

"This is where we live, Lacey," Carin said evenly. "We were only staying at Nathan's while I was recovering."

"You're not recovered yet." Lacey apparently had no rule about not arguing.

"I'm recovered enough. Aren't I, Nathan?" Carin's gaze went straight to Nathan, challenging him to back her up.

He shoved his hands into the pockets of his canvas shorts. "If you say so."

"I say so," Carin said. "And that is that."

She'd known she was living dangerously all the time she'd been at Nathan's. But it was true, what he'd said—she hadn't had any choice. Not a viable choice, anyway.

She couldn't make Lacey take care of her. She couldn't impose on Estelle or Fiona or Hugh. And until she'd been able to hobble around, staying in her own place—even with help—would have been difficult in the extreme.

So she'd stayed at Nathan's. And she'd steeled herself against him as best she could. It had been hard once she'd begun to feel better, once her mind had become less preoccupied with pain and more with the persistent presence of Nathan Wolfe.

As soon as she could put weight on her leg, she'd refused to let him carry her—even though she nearly went stir crazy staying in the house. He'd offered several times to carry her down to the beach.

"You can sit on a towel on the sand and watch Lacey swim," he'd said.

And it had been very tempting. It would have got her out of the house. It would have permitted her some time on the beach. It would have been lovely to sit in the sun and watch Lacey swim.

But she would have been in Nathan's arms all the way

there and all the way back. *And* she would have had to watch Nathan swim.

It was bad enough seeing Nathan in shorts and T-shirts every day. With the heat, there was rarely any reason for him to wear more than that. But if she'd taken him up on his offer to go to the beach with them, she would have seen him in less.

She had enough trouble remaining indifferent to Nathan. She didn't need to see his hard abs and bare chest. She didn't need to watch his bathing trunks mold to his masculine frame and watch water stream down his belly and disappear into his trunks. She had enough memories. She didn't need that!

The night before she'd packed up and made Maurice come and get her, she hadn't been able to sleep because of those memories. They'd had her shifting around on her bed, agitated and uncomfortable. It was too hot, she'd told herself. It was too humid. There were half a dozen reasons why she couldn't sleep.

Finally she'd got up to use the bathroom and get a drink of water. Ordinarily when she did so, she tried to get from her room to the bathroom as quickly and quietly as possible.

Last night she'd been quiet, but she hadn't moved quickly enough. The moonlight had tempted her to slow down as she passed the archway to the living room. And a glimpse of the sculpted masculine form sprawled on the sofa had immediately drawn her eye, had made her pause and stare.

The silvery light streaming in the window highlighted the planes and threw into shadow the angles of Nathan's muscular body. He was lying on his back, his only covering a pair of light-colored loose-fitting boxer shorts. But their looseness didn't completely mask the swell of his masculinity.

Carin couldn't help herself. She stopped. She looked. And then Nathan had moved and spoken to her.

Dear God, he'd been awake! He'd seen her standing there ogling him!

At least he'd only thought she needed help! Quickly Carin had assured him she was fine and had limped rapidly away.

That had been bad. What had followed was worse.

If she had been restless before her trek down the hall, after Nathan had spoken to her, Carin hadn't been able to sleep at all. She'd been awake and staring out into the moonlight through the sliding glass door to her bedroom when another door had opened and she saw Nathan, still wearing only his boxers, step out onto the deck.

As she watched, he had grabbed one of the towels hung out to dry on the railing. Then, slinging it around his neck, he hurried down the steps and in seconds had disappeared through the trees onto the path that led to the beach.

He was going for a swim? At two-thirty in the morning?

Why? Because he was as restless as she was? Because he was remembering things, too?

It was possible. It was even likely. She didn't question that he was still attracted to her. She didn't doubt that he'd be delighted to go to bed with her. He just wouldn't love her.

Carin wanted love.

But three-quarters of an hour later, when she saw him come out of the trees and into the clearing wearing nothing but the towel around his shoulders, she found herself tempted to settle for less.

Dear God, he was beautiful.

She would love to paint him, to capture the hard lines of his body silvered in the moonlight, to catch his catlike grace as he strode across the grass and mounted the steps. But more than that she wanted to touch him, to feel once more the strength and hardness of his body beneath her fingers. She wanted to run her hands over his hair-roughened skin. She wanted to trace the line of his jaw with her lips. She wanted to touch them to his chest, to kiss her way down the arrow of hair that ran down the middle of it, that arrowed directly toward his very visible masculinity.

She wanted to touch him there.

Carin sucked in a sharp breath at the heat in her own body, at its readiness to know him fully, to let him touch her!

Love.

She wanted *love,* she reminded herself.

And that's when she knew that come daybreak she had to move out.

Living dangerously was one thing. But she was in danger of crossing the line from dangerous to foolish.

Because it would be foolish indeed—as well as all too easy—to settle for sex with Nathan Wolfe.

CHAPTER EIGHT

THE BANGING on the front door woke her. Carin struggled up, dazed, then worried. It was just past seven. Who would be knocking at this hour?

All she could think was that something had happened to Miss Saffron. The old lady didn't have a phone. Maybe she'd fallen and someone had found her and needed to call Doc Rasmussen. She fumbled into her robe, cursed her cast and, not even bothering to comb her hair, she hurried down the stairs and jerked open the door.

It was Nathan. He grinned at her.

Carin stared, nonplussed, aware of her uncombed hair and hastily donned robe in the face of his freshly shaved bright-eyed face. ''Nathan? I thought—'' She dragged a hand through her hair. ''What are you doing here?''

''Picking up Lacey.''

''Now? It's seven o'clock! She's not even up.''

''Well, if you were at my house, I could have woken her and you wouldn't be bothered.''

He was baiting her, Carin knew. She deliberately didn't respond to it. ''I'll get her up. You can come back later.''

Instead he stepped past her into the living room. ''No problem. I'll have a cup of coffee while I'm waiting.''

''I didn't make coffee this morning.'' Carin followed him into the kitchen, wishing she could just grab him by the collar and throw him back out the door. It had been bad enough being around Nathan at his place. There, at least, the rooms were big enough that it didn't seem as if they were on top of each other. Here it did. As he got out coffee mugs, then turned to look in the other cupboard for the coffee, he literally brushed right against her. Carin jumped back.

Nathan didn't even seem to notice. "You want a cup, too?" He found the coffee and began measuring it into the coffeepot.

"No, I do not." She glared at him. "I'm going up to get dressed."

"Don't bother on my account." He gave her a grin that had the effect of annoying her even more.

She banged on Lacey's door, then took refuge in her room. It took her a long time to get dressed, partly because the cast made things difficult and partly because she was so flustered that she couldn't seem to manage to button her shorts or do something with her hair. Ordinarily she would have asked for Lacey's help. But she wasn't going to ask this morning.

If she did, no doubt Nathan would be the one to button her shorts or braid her hair!

Besides, she decided, if she took enough time he and Lacey would be gone before she came back downstairs again. In fact, it was true.

A few minutes passed and Lacey clattered downstairs, a few more and she'd obviously grabbed breakfast because she sang out, "See you later, Mom!"

"See you later," Carin called back and breathed a sigh of relief.

Five hours later Nathan was back.

"We ran into Thomas and Lorenzo at the dive shop when we got back," he said. "She went off with them. So I brought lunch."

"I don't need you bringing lunch." Carin said testily as he came in carrying a bag that she recognized as being full of conch fritters. Her mouth watered. Her stomach growled.

"Thank you, Nathan. I'm really glad you thought of me sitting here by myself with no food in the house," he said in a mock falsetto as he walked right past her into the kitchen and began opening her cabinets.

"I do, too, have food in the house!"

"Not according to Lacey." He got out plates, set them on the table, opened a drawer, took out silverware and began dishing up lunch.

Lacey was a traitor, Carin thought grimly. They had *some* food in the house, and Maurice would have gone shopping for her.

"Lacey is a picky eater," she grumbled.

"Good thing you're not," Nathan said cheerfully. "Otherwise these conch fritters and cole slaw would be going to waste." He plunked several fritters on her plate and added a dollop of cole slaw alongside them, then sat down and began to eat.

He was back again at dinner. And the next day it was exactly the same. She might as well not have moved out at all. Nathan was bound and determined to make them dependent on him.

Lacey was already under his spell. And Carin knew that she only had so much resistance. If he kept this up, she was afraid she would be in danger of succumbing.

She couldn't allow it!

And she could just sit here and hope that his work would take him away. Undoubtedly eventually it would—but not soon enough.

So if he wouldn't leave, she would.

She had told Stacia she wasn't coming to New York, but now it sounded like a very good idea.

It would be a treat for Lacey, who had been all for it from the moment the show had been proposed. It would make Stacia happy. And given what—or rather, who—she was facing here, dealing with millions of New Yorkers seemed far less stressful.

She called Stacia and said she would come.

"Well, you've seen sense at last. Hooray. I'll make the arrangements."

"Wonderful. Thanks." She didn't say a word about Nathan.

She didn't say a word *to* Nathan, either.

She didn't want him deciding to come along. This was her trip—hers and Lacey's. And if she felt the tiniest bit guilty because his photos were in the show, too—and had in fact saved the show for her—well, he'd had other shows, and she needed some space.

She didn't even say anything to Lacey about the trip. She didn't want her telling Nathan. Besides, she wanted it to be a surprise.

She only told Hugh because she needed him to take them to Nassau. "Bright and early Monday morning," she said.

She didn't say they needed to leave early because she wanted to be gone before Nathan showed up.

On Monday morning she got Lacey up early.

"It's barely six," Lacey grumbled. "Dad didn't say he was coming early today."

"It's nothing to do with your father," Carin said. "Come on. Get up. It's a surprise."

Lacey rubbed her eyes, looking disgruntled, then curious. "A suprise? What kind of surprise?" But she was dragging herself out of bed.

"You'll see."

Now that they were actually going, Carin was feeling excited, too. She'd packed a bag for each of them last night after Lacey was asleep, then called Fiona and asked her to feed Zeno while they were gone.

Now, when Lacey came downstairs and saw the bags sitting by the door, she looked at her mother, wide-eyed. "We're going on a trip? Where are we going? Are we going to New York?"

"Wait and see," Carin said, smiling, as Hugh pulled up out front.

"Are we going to Nassau?" Lacey pressed.

"You'll see," Carin said. "You'll love it."

But she had no idea how thrilled Lacey would be—or how shocked *she* would be—when they got to the landing field and Nathan was standing by the helicopter, grinning at them!

Carin opened her mouth as he opened the door of Hugh's car and winked at her.

"No arguments. Not in front of Lacey."

It had been sheer luck that Stacia had called his place to talk to Carin about the arrangements for the trip to New York. Obviously, she'd thought Carin and Lacey were still living with him.

"Trip?" Nathan had echoed when she'd rung.

"For the opening. It's next week, you know. I was badgering her to come and she kept saying no. Then, all of a sudden she finally said yes. I suppose," she'd added, "I have you to thank for that."

Very likely, yes, Nathan thought grimly.

"She didn't mention if you were coming, too," Stacia went on. "Are you?"

"I am." Oh, yes.

"Wonderful. I told her I'd make arrangements for a place to stay and—"

"Not necessary. We'll be staying with my family."

"Oh, of course. That will be lovely for you." Stacia's tone told him how delighted she was.

Nathan doubted Carin would feel the same.

She hadn't argued with him in front of Lacey, but she hadn't exactly been sweetness and light personified since then, either.

Lacey had been delighted enough not to notice that her mother was grinding her teeth.

Nathan had noticed. He'd noticed, too, that she'd deliberately ignored him, clambering into the helicopter to sit on the seat next to Hugh's dog, Belle, his "copilot," leaving Nathan to sit with Lacey in the back.

He didn't mind sitting with Lacey. His daughter's enthusiasm delighted him and, as far as Nathan was concerned, it justified what he'd done, arranging things without Carin's knowledge. She wouldn't have agreed if he'd told her—and it was all too clear how happy Lacey was.

As the helicopter lifted off, she was practically bouncing off the seat in her excitement.

"See! There's the school! And our house, and Lorenzo's, and Maurice and Estelle's! Oh, look! We're going to see your place!" She gave another bounce as Hugh aimed the copter toward the seaward side of the island. "See it, Dad? Mom? Do you see?"

"I see," Nathan said.

Carin glanced that way, but she didn't say anything. She sat, stiff and unyielding all the way to Nassau, her good arm wrapped around Belle.

So much for taking charge and controlling her own destiny. So much for putting space between them. So much for the trip for two—just her and Lacey—to New York.

Of course Nathan was coming along because Stacia—of all people!—had called him and asked if he was coming. Naturally he'd said he was. And because he was Nathan, naturally he'd told Stacia not to bother making arrangements, that he would handle that end of things.

"Handle them how?" Carin asked.

"Well, we can't go to a hotel," he said practically. "My brothers would be offended."

And Carin knew without asking that Nathan had no intention of staying in a hotel no matter how much she argued, which she couldn't do anyway since Lacey was sitting next to her, all ears.

"Don't say we're going to stay with Dominic."

The very thought appalled her. Stay with the man she'd jilted? Talk about uncomfortable situations.

"No. His place isn't really big enough. We're going to stay with Rhys and Mariah."

Carin barely remembered Rhys, though she felt pretty sure he would remember her. "He's married again?" She knew his first wife had died.

"To Mariah. She's Sierra's sister. You'll like her."

"Does she have purple hair, too?" Lacey asked avidly. She thought Sierra's purple locks were absolutely fascinating.

Carin thought they were pretty amazing, too. She still found it hard to believe that Sierra, with her purple hair and funky day-glo clothes, was Dominic's wife. But they'd certainly seemed deeply in love when she'd met them on the island last autumn.

"I don't know what color it is now," Nathan answered Lacey. "You'll have to wait and see. Dominic's picking us up."

It should have been horrible.

In scant moments she was going to be face-to-face with the man she'd jilted. She'd seen him before—twice—but both times had been on Pelican Cay. She'd never presumed to set foot on his turf. And even though Dominic had professed to have forgiven her, who knew what he really felt? And would he and his wife really want to welcome her into their home?

Carin knew Sierra was "unusual." But did her unusualness extend to welcoming her husband's ex-fiancée? Carin tried to imagine and couldn't. Why on earth couldn't Nathan have left well enough alone?

"I've got your tote bag," Nathan said over his shoulder, steering Lacey ahead of him and checking behind him to make sure Carin was following as they disembarked. As if she might duck out and vanish given a chance.

If it weren't for Lacey, she would have been tempted. She didn't want to have to smile and make small talk with Dominic. She didn't want to go back to his Fifth Avenue apartment and act like she was glad to be there.

What she wanted was to strangle Nathan for forcing her into this.

But she couldn't, she thought grimly. Not in front of Lacey.

The next thing she knew Dominic was striding toward them, his hard face lightened by a broad grin and his whole tough demeanor softened by the baby girl he held in one arm. He gave Nathan a punch on the shoulder, then wrapped his free arm around his brother's neck and gave it a friendly squeeze.

"Took your own sweet time coming to see us, didn't you, bro?" When he released Nathan, he wrapped Lacey in a one-armed hug and said, "My God, you're like a weed. You've grown a foot since spring." And then he released her and looked at Carin, smiling still as he held out a hand to her. "Welcome home."

It had been years since Carin had thought of New York City as home. And yet Dominic was right. She'd felt that eager longing prick her as the city had come into view. She'd been like Lacey as they'd left Pelican Cay, her eyes seeking landmarks, feeling a sense of connection and remembrance. She'd been barely more than a child when she'd been here last. But the city would always be a part of her.

She was grateful to Dominic for recognizing that. Now she took the hand he offered and met his eyes. "Thank you. It's good to be here." And as she said the words, she felt the tightness in her chest ease. She wasn't lying as she'd thought she would have to.

"Meet my baby girl," Dominic said, a father's deep quiet pride in his voice as he held out his daughter. "This is Lily."

"She's absolutely beautiful, Dominic," Carin said, and meant that, too.

Lily, who was probably four or five months old, looked a great deal like Lacey had at that age. She had lots of straight dark hair and deep-blue eyes just like her father's and uncle's. She studied Carin seriously.

"Hello, Lily," Carin said gravely and reached out a finger to stroke the little girl's hand. Lily's fingers wrapped around hers. She had a fierce grip.

"Can I carry her?" Lacey asked. "I've never had a cousin before."

Dominic grinned and, easing his daughter's grasp from around Carin's finger, he handed the little girl over to Lacey. "She wiggles. Hang on tight."

"I will." Lacey said the words as if they were a vow and took her little cousin from Dominic's arms.

Seeing the two together, Carin felt a pang of longing that caught her unprepared. The sight of another child like Lacey forced her to recall long-ago hopes and dreams of more children, of brothers and sisters, not only cousins, for Lacey to grow up with.

A quick look at Nathan told her that he was aware of how alike they were, as well. His eyes went from the girls to Carin. They challenged her with everything she'd once thought she wanted.

It was a relief when Dominic said, "Come on. Let's go. Sierra's home fixing supper. She'll be waiting."

Carin's worries about Sierra were unfounded. The younger woman welcomed them like long-lost friends.

"Oh, good! You're finally here!" She hugged Lacey and Carin exuberantly, then held Lacey out at arm's length and said, "You and Lily could be sisters." She sounded so pleased with the notion that Carin relaxed a bit more.

And when Sierra pushed her into an overstuffed chair overlooking Central Park, handed her a glass of wine and said, "Take it easy. You've still got an arm in a cast. You must be exhausted. You need to chill,'' Carin felt herself doing just that. She settled back, relaxed and actually found herself feeling at home.

Dominic and Sierra's Fifth Avenue apartment, which she had imagined would be a steel-and-glass palace, was far more comfortable and casual than Carin would have expected. It had to be worth millions, had at least ten rooms, four of them with huge windows overlooking Central Park. And yet it felt warm and welcoming with its red oak woodwork, overstuffed furniture and live foliage. Was that a real tree? By golly, it was!

Carin felt as if she were in a treehouse. And when she said so, Sierra laughed. ''Yes, the place is a holdover from Dominic's Tarzan days.''

''I like it,'' Carin said.

And Sierra nodded. ''I do, too. It's why I married him.''

Carin goggled, then realized that Sierra was kidding. It was hard to imagine anyone being able to joke about Dominic Wolfe. She certainly never could have. She was glad he had found Sierra.

She was amazed to find her own painting of Pelican Cay in the living room. She'd have expected abstract art, but instead the walls contained homely primitive paintings of the Wolfes' house in Pelican Cay and her own watercolor of the village from the custom house dock.

Now, catching Carin looking at her painting, Sierra grinned. ''It's my favorite,'' she said, ''because it captures the island so well. And because it reminds me of the day Dominic and I finally began to understand and trust each other—thanks to you.''

Her smile was so warm and friendly that Carin felt as if she were being praised for something she hadn't really done. She shrugged. ''I'm glad you like it.''

''Mariah does, too. I told her she needs to buy one of the island at your show.''

"I'll give her one. I wanted to give you and Dominic that one."

But Dominic had insisted on paying her—had, in fact, tried to give her more than she'd been asking, telling her she'd given him something worth far more than her painting.

Knowledge at last of why she'd jilted him, he'd meant. And when he'd come down in the spring he'd told her that meeting her and Lacey had opened communications between him and Sierra as well. Carin was delighted that they were so happy together. Watching him now, doting on his baby daughter, she couldn't help but smile.

The doorbell rang just then, and when Sierra opened the door more Wolfes spilled into the apartment.

Carin immediately identified Rhys, a slightly harder-edged, more muscular version of Nathan and Dominic. Rhys was a member of an elite corps of firefighters who traveled the globe putting out oil and industrial fires. With him was a stunning, dark-haired woman almost as tall as he was. Something about her eyes and her smile looked familiar. Then Carin remembered that she was Sierra's sister. She and Rhys were each carrying a child.

"Look, Mom. More cousins!" Lacey was beaming.

"Come meet the rest of the family," Nathan said and, snagging Carin's hand, drew her to her feet to introduce her to Rhys's wife and his twins, Stephen and Elizabeth.

Rhys gave her a hug, and Mariah did, too.

"Hugs," Elizabeth demanded. And Carin gave her one, too. And Stephen demanded a kiss, which he got.

"Lucky guy," Nathan said. "It's more than she'll give me."

"You gotta learn how to ask," Rhys said with a grin.

Carin had hoped she would be able to remain quietly aloof. There was no reason for her to get involved. It was fine for Lacey to be included. But this was Nathan's family, not hers.

Try telling the Wolfes that.

They didn't believe in aloof. Not even Nathan, the quietest of the brothers, was quiet tonight.

Put the three brothers together and the noise level rose exponentially. There was immediate talk of the Yankees and the Mets. Discussion of soccer and diving. Dominic and Rhys wanted Nathan to go to a ball game. Rhys and Nathan wanted Dominic to take time off to go fishing.

"You wouldn't think Nathan came to work," Sierra said.

"All they do is talk about fishing," Mariah agreed.

Sierra rolled her eyes. "Come on." She grabbed Carin and hauled her into the kitchen. "You can supervise me making a salad."

"Or a mess," Mariah said. "And we can warn you about getting involved with a Wolfe."

"I'm not involved with a Wolfe," Carin protested.

"Yeah, right." Mariah obviously didn't believe that for a minute. She put the lasagna she'd brought into the oven to heat it.

"You just keep thinking that and you won't know what hit you," Sierra agreed as she tore up lettuce and tossed it in a bowl. "They get what they want, those Wolfe boys."

"Nathan doesn't," Carin said firmly.

Both sisters looked at her, then at each other. "Maybe we're just pushovers," Mariah said to her sister. "Too easy. We should be tougher. Like Carin. After all Carin dumped your husband."

"I didn't—" Carin's face flamed. "I mean—"

"Jilted him, then," Sierra said, calling a spade a spade. "Sounds to me like he deserved it. And he didn't deserve you."

"Whereas," Mariah said dryly, "he definitely deserves Sierra!"

Sierra gave a wicked grin and chuckled in a way that made Carin laugh, too.

"The question is," Mariah said, "does Nathan deserve Carin?"

They both looked at her. "Does he?" Sierra asked.

"We're not—I don't—" Carin stopped, at a loss to explain.

"He has asked you to marry him, hasn't he?" Sierra stopped tearing lettuce and fixed Carin with a steady gaze.

"Yes, but—"

"You need to make him pay first," Mariah finished for her.

"I—"

"But then you need to marry him," Sierra said. "Because he's Lacey's father."

"I don't—"

"And you love him," Mariah said quietly.

Carin opened her mouth to deny it, but the words wouldn't come. They all looked at each other, the truth settling in.

Then suddenly Rhys appeared in the doorway with a twin in each arm. "They're starving. They're starting to chew on the furniture. When's dinner?"

"Coming right up," Sierra answered for her sister. "Go wash up. There's the bell again. Tell Dominic to answer the door," she added as the bell rang. "That'll be Douglas." Then when Rhys left, she turned her gaze on Carin again.

"Don't waste your love," she said. "It's too precious."

"Rhys almost blew it," Mariah added. "But finally he came around."

"And so did Dominic. You have to start somewhere," Sierra agreed.

"Ah, there they are!" Nathan's father, Douglas, appeared, beaming in the doorway. "The three most beautiful women in the world!"

He kissed each of his daughters-in-law, and then he kissed Carin, stepped back, paused and held her cheeks between his palms. "Ah, Carin. When are you going to make an honest man out of that son of mine?"

"Dad!" Nathan came up behind him and got a headlock on his old man. "Leave the poor woman alone."

"I was only asking," Douglas protested, slipping out of Nathan's grasp. "Just want her to know we're all for it. You do know that, don't you, Carin?"

Carin flushed. "Yes, Mr., er…yes, Douglas."

"Dad sounds better, don't you think?" He winked.

"I'm capable of doing my own proposing," Nathan said through his teeth.

Douglas turned his gaze on his son. "But are you capable of getting her to say yes?"

A tide of red washed above the collar of Nathan's shirt. "You'll just have to wait and see, won't you?"

"No fighting in my kitchen." Sierra advanced on them with a stirring spoon. "Out! Both of you." She thrust a handful of silverware at her father-in-law. "Make yourself useful. Set the table."

"Douglas has a subtle touch, doesn't he?" Mariah said with a grin.

"Oh, yes," Sierra agreed. They looked at each other and laughed. Then they grinned at Carin.

"He's very fond of you," Mariah told her.

"I jilted his son."

"But you gave him a granddaughter. That cancels things out."

Carin wasn't sure she believed that. But Douglas certainly did have a soft spot for Lacey. And, happily, he didn't say anything more during dinner about her getting together with Nathan.

Neither did anyone else. The talk was easy and general, and Carin let it wash over her as she listened to the various threads of conversation—the merits of a particular Yankee pitcher, the latest rock star Mariah had interviewed, the best fishing spots on the north shore of Long Island, whether or not Lily was teething—and enjoyed it all in spite of herself.

This was the sort of family she'd always dreamed of having.

An only child raised by a widowed father who had more time and interest for his business than he'd ever had for her, Carin had always dreamed of being a part of a family like this. When she'd agreed with her father's estimation of Dominic as a good potential husband, it had been in part because she knew he had brothers and she'd hoped to become part of his family circle.

Of course she'd ruined that herself. And since then she'd learned that families could be created by love and effort, that the same blood didn't have to run in people's veins to make them family.

She had her own "created family" on the island. Maurice and Estelle included her and Lacey in their holiday gatherings. And in the past few years she and Hugh and a few of the other young unattached people on Pelican Cay had created a family of sorts.

But those "families," wonderful though they were, didn't yet have much history—not like the Wolfe brothers, who were, even in the middle of a lovely dinner, reminiscing about baseball games of their youth and whose bike had popped a tire at an inopportune moment and which brother caught the biggest fish the last time they were all at Pelican Cay, and not like Mariah and Sierra, who shared a history, too.

How wonderful it would have been to have had a family who would share such memories.

Even as she thought it, Carin watched Lacey's expressions as she listened to her father and her uncles teasing and battling and arguing with each other. Her daughter's gaze went from one to the other, as if she was watching a tennis match. And all the while she was grinning so much her smile seemed to wrap two times around her face.

Carin tried to remember the last time Lacey had looked that happy.

It was the night she'd come back from Nathan's—the day he'd arrived—when she knew at last that her father loved her and that he'd come to Pelican Cay determined to make her part of his life.

Oh, Lacey.

"Tell me about your accident," Douglas requested, interrupting Carin's thoughts. "Nathan said he was terrified when you went over the handlebars. He thought you'd killed yourself."

She dragged her gaze away from Lacey's face. "I should have been going slower. I had to swerve when Zeno ran in front of me."

"Zeno?" Douglas's brows hiked. "You have a wolf on the island?"

"Not a wolf. A dog."

And so they talked about Zeno. And about her show. About her painting and who was handling the business while she was here.

Douglas said he was thrilled that she and Nathan were going to be part of this show together. But he didn't take advantage of the subject to ask her again when she was going to marry his son. He just talked about Nathan's photography, about how well Nathan was doing, about how proud he was of him.

Dominic poured more wine in everyone's glasses. Lacey took the twins out into the living room and built block towers with them. Rhys challenged Nathan to a game of pool.

Dominic tapped Carin on the shoulder. "The old man must be boring you by now. How about coming to talk to me while I clean up in the kitchen?"

"He wasn't—" Carin began to protest.

But Douglas stood up. "Yes, yes. You go on with Dominic. Don't let an old windbag waste your time."

"You didn't want to hear him sing Nathan's praises anyway, did you?" Dominic asked her.

Carin stammered, unsure how to answer that.

Dominic just laughed. "Come along."

If anyone had told her that she would ever stand in Dominic Wolfe's kitchen, talking to him while he loaded the dishwasher, she would have said they were insane. Not even when she had been going to marry Dominic had she considered that he would unbend that far. But he acted as if he was no stranger to dirty plates and pots and pans.

And while he did it, he talked about Pelican Cay, about going back there with Sierra. "I was scared to," he said.

"Scared?" Carin blinked, surprised at the confidence he was sharing.

Dominic shrugged. "It was sex at first, you know, between us. At least that's all we thought it was. But it wasn't just sex for long. It was Sierra. I cared a lot about her. I *loved* her. But I didn't know how she felt." There was still a raw aching sound in his voice when he spoke of those days.

"She loves you," Carin said quickly, trying to reassure him. Any fool could see that.

Dominic grinned. "I know that now."

"I'm glad," she told him sincerely. "I'm glad you're happy. I worried about it. About you. But I couldn't—"

"I know you couldn't marry me. It's a good thing you didn't. I just wish you could have told me why. I wish I'd *let* you tell me why." His mouth twisted wryly. But then he shrugged and smiled again, though his eyes grew serious. "I hope you and Nathan can be happy, too."

Carin wet her lips. What could she say to that? It wasn't the same as with him and Sierra.

"I hope so, too," she said at last.

It was close to midnight by the time they went home with Rhys and Mariah and the twins. Stephen and Lizzie were both asleep, and Lacey was yawning madly as Rhys flagged down two taxis and directed them to their brown-stone across the park.

"I don't want to inconvenience you," Carin began.

"You won't," Rhys said flatly, "unless you make me take you down to midtown to some hotel."

Carin sighed and settled back against the seat, once more giving in to the inevitable, "I won't do that."

Rhys and Mariah owned the whole brownstone they lived in. They had two tenants on the upper floors, but the third-floor studio apartment that looked out onto the garden was vacant.

"We keep it for friends," Mariah said as she led Carin and Lacey up the stairs. Nathan had been deputized to help Rhys get the two sleeping children into their beds. "And brothers. And their families."

"I'm not family," Carin protested.

"I am," Lacey said firmly.

"Of course you are," Mariah said. "And Nathan is."

"*Nathan*?"

"Oh, dear. I just assumed... Would you rather Nathan slept downstairs with us."

"We stayed with him when Mom got hurt," Lacey said. "He slept on the couch right by her room. He carried her to the bathroom every day," she told her aunt Mariah.

After that revelation, Carin could hardly say she wanted him downstairs. "It's all right," Carin mumbled.

And then she discovered the sleeping arrangements.

It was a one-room apartment. The "sofa" was a trundle bed and there was a high built-in queen-size platform bed which was separated from the rest of the room by the two-foot high carpeted "wall" that enclosed two sides of it, giving only the illusion of privacy.

When Nathan finally came upstairs half an hour later, Carin had done the best she could.

Lacey, in pajamas, was tucked into the platform bed. The trundle was made up for Nathan.

"I'll just slip in alongside Lacey," Carin told him. At least they would have the two-foot wall between them.

"With your arm?"

Oh, hell. She hadn't even thought of that. She was so used to her cast by now that she barely gave it any thought. It was an inconvenience to her. But it would be more than that to Lacey, who was a restless sleeper. Lacey would be banging into her all night.

"I'll pull out the other trundle bed for you," Nathan offered with a grin.

He did—and lined it up right next to his. The room was now virtually a wall-to-wall bed—with Carin right next to Nathan.

"Isn't this cozy?" He grinned.

Carin gave him a hard look and didn't deign to reply.

"I think it's cool." Lacey shoved herself up on her pillow and peered over the little wall. "I know you said I was going to get a surprise," she said to her mother, eyes shining. "But this is so cool. All of us being here together like a real family." Lacey's gaze went from Carin to Nathan. "This is the best surprise ever."

CHAPTER NINE

OF ALL THE WOLFE BROTHERS, Nathan was the born fisherman.

Dominic and Rhys were fast-moving, take-charge, do-it-now men who gnashed their teeth if the fish weren't biting. They fished, but mostly they argued about where they ought to be fishing, what kind of bait to use, what time to go out, when to come in, and which one had caught the bigger fish.

The fact was, Nathan almost always caught the biggest fish because he was the one with the patience. He was the one who studied the currents, checked the depth, considered the temperature and the time of year and made his plans accordingly.

And then he sat. And sat. And sat.

He always knew what he was after, and he was always willing to wait. A guy didn't value something unless he worked for it, Nathan figured. And he valued it even more if he'd endured some hardship and frustration along the way.

What was true of fishing was also true of his photography and his books. They were products of much thought, long hours, vast patience and hard work.

So was courting Carin.

And if thought, long hours, vast patience and a fair amount of work had anything to do with it, the way Nathan figured it, he ought to value Carin more than anything or anyone on earth.

Talk about patience, endurance, frustration! God Almighty!

Here he was in bed lying mere inches from her—*inches!*—and she was sound asleep.

Carin wasn't frustrated. Not a bit! She had glared at him as if he'd manipulated the whole disastrous sleeping arrangements bit, then she'd brushed her teeth, kissed Lacey good-night, and climbed into the trundle bed right next to his as if she didn't even notice him.

So what else was new? Nathan thought, grinding his teeth.

He'd done his damnedest to make this evening a success, to make her enjoy herself, to encourage her to feel a part of the family—and what did he have to show for it?

Zip. Nada. Zilch. Not a damn thing.

Unless you counted the fact that she was now comfortable enough around him to fall asleep virtually in the same bed with him as if he weren't even there! Lots of comfort in that revelation, huh? Nathan practically snorted in disgust.

She'd spent the whole evening basically ignoring him. She'd seemed to enjoy his sisters-in-law. She'd played with his nieces and nephew. She'd chatted easily with his father and Rhys. She'd even gone off into the kitchen and, he hoped, had a heart-to-heart with Dominic. But had it done any good?

God knew.

Nathan certainly didn't. She was acting as if he wasn't even here.

Maybe he should have told her he was coming along. Oh, yeah, that would have done a lot of good. She'd have refused to come, point-blank. No, it was better he hadn't said anything. Better just to go on with events as planned—and hope that she eventually softened toward him, trusted him. Loved him.

But every time he hoped, every time he thought things would go his way, every time he thought he had come up with the perfect bait, Carin looked at it, swam lazily around, daring him to hope. And then…she turned away.

Nathan was a good fisherman. He was a determined fisherman. But a guy had his limits. He didn't remember Carin being so stubborn.

He didn't remember her being so beautiful! But then, she was only inches away, so close he could feel the heat of her body. A sigh shuddered through him.

He didn't know how long he could last.

"Dad?" Lacey's whisper cut into the silence, surprising him. She'd been so tired he thought she'd be asleep before they shut out the lights.

He rolled to a sitting position. "What?"

Her head appeared above the little wall. "Just checking." Her grin flashed in the moonlight. "I woke up and thought I'd dreamed it. But it's true. We're really here."

"Oh, yeah," Nathan muttered. "We're really here."

"Good." She sighed contentedly. Her head disappeared again and she settled back against the pillows. "G'night, Dad."

"G'night, Lace."

"Dad?"

"Hmm?"

"I hope it's always like this."

God help him, Nathan thought.

Carin wished it could always be like this.

Well, not the going-to-bed with Nathan just inches away. At least, not if she had to resist him. That was hard. And it didn't get any easier with each night that passed.

But the rest of the time was far more wonderful than she ever could have dreamed. She'd envisioned a happy little trip for herself and Lacey, a chance to sightsee, the possibility of visiting some of the places she'd known growing up, to show Lacey a little of her history.

But this was so much more.

And they owed it all to Nathan.

One more way in which she was beholden to Nathan.

The list went on and on. She didn't want to feel grateful. But on Lacey's behalf, she had to be.

Lacey was having a wonderful time. Sierra, with Lily in tow, took her up to see Uncle Dominic in his office the first day, while Nathan and Carin went to the gallery to talk to Stacia. From there, Lacey told her, they all—Dominic included—went sightseeing. They took a boat trip around Manhattan Island. They saw so many things Lacey couldn't remember them all. She was delighted—as much because she'd enjoyed the day with her uncle, aunt and cousin as because of where they went.

The next day Mariah and Rhys and Douglas took Lacey and the twins to the zoo and to Central Park. Lacey loved it—mostly loved *them*.

"I wish they would all come to Pelican Cay," she told Carin and Nathan that evening. "They can come soon, can't they?"

"Sure," Nathan said easily.

And Carin smiled, pained and pleased at the same time. "Of course."

Her own days had been as memorable as Lacey's—in a far different way. Stacia had asked her and Nathan to come down to the gallery to supervise the hanging of the paintings and photos and to meet with a couple of interviewers. She had been nervous, never having done anything on this scale before.

But Stacia made it easy. And Nathan made it an experience she would never forget. In the gallery she saw the professional Nathan Wolfe. She knew he had an eye for a good photo, but now she saw that he had an eye, too, for how those photos—and her paintings—ought to be displayed.

He countered Stacia's idea of just having their work in the same gallery and dealing with the same island with his own notion that the paintings and photos ought to work together, side by side, complementing and contrasting with each other, offering two perspectives on island life.

"Island Eyes, isn't that what you want?" he said to Stacia.

"But you don't know what paintings I've done," Carin said.

In fact, it seemed that he did. While she'd been laid up, he had helped Stacia pack and ship all her work. He'd taken photos of them. And then he'd gone out and shot pictures that would echo and complement her paintings.

As Stacia and the gallery personnel hung them, with Nathan's help, Carin sat back and stared. It was like seeing her vision amplified, developed, shaded, sharpened. Each of her paintings became a focal point, heightened by Nathan's work—and Lacey's—which surrounded it.

Carin was amazed at the quality of Lacey's work.

"She's good," Nathan said simply. He had picked half a dozen of their daughter's photos to use in the show and had matted and framed them himself.

"With Lacey's help," he told Carin. "That's what we were doing some of the mornings when we were gone."

"Does she know they're going to be up?" she asked.

He shook his head and smiled. "One more little surprise."

Lacey would be over the moon. Carin felt a lump grow in her throat.

One more thing they owed Nathan.

The third day—the day of the opening—Sierra came over and fixed both Carin's hair and Lacey's.

"Will you dye it blue?" Lacey begged. "Or purple? Like yours was."

Sierra's was a natural brown now. She'd stopped using dyes, she told Lacey, when she found out she was pregnant with Lily.

Now she wouldn't dye Lacey's hair, either. "It's too

beautiful a color the way it is," she said. "Like a beautiful sorrel. But I can add some beads."

Lacey's eyes widened. "Really? My friend Marisa has beads."

In minutes, so did Lacey. Sierra braided a few strands of multi-colored beads into Lacey's hair, giving it an unexpected flair, and making her niece grin and shake her head every time she came to a mirror.

"You look great," Sierra said. "And so do you," she told Carin.

Carin was pretty sure she was being kind. Of course her hair was fine, because Sierra had done it that afternoon. And her dress was lovely, because Mariah and Sierra had picked it out.

They'd taken her shopping last night, and while Carin had wanted to opt for a basic black conservative dress, they wouldn't hear of it.

"You want to look like you're going to an undertakers' convention?" Sierra demanded.

"Black is supposed to look arty," Carin said in a voice barely above a whisper.

"How much black do you normally wear?" Mariah asked.

"Not much."

"Well, there you are. Your dress should reflect who you are."

So she'd ended up with a casually sophisticated dress in a myriad of blues and greens, fitted at the bodice, nipped in at the waist, and flared so that it looked like the sea swirling around her knees when she walked.

"Island colors," Sierra said approvingly.

"And a style that shows off her tan," Mariah had agreed.

It showed way more tan than Carin thought appropriate. Only the thinnest straps held it up. And besides giving the world a look at Carin's tanned shoulders, it showed off most of her back. There was a good deal more to look at than the white plaster on her arm.

Nathan, who was waiting in Mariah and Rhys's apartment, goggled when she come downstairs wearing it.

"Turn around," Mariah commanded.

Carin did. And Nathan swallowed visibly when he saw the plunging back.

"That?" he said hoarsely. "You're wearing *that*?"

Nervous already, Carin managed, "Is it too…?"

But the fact was she could hardly speak for staring, too. She'd never seen Nathan dressed up before. He'd been appealing in scruffy shorts and T-shirts, but in a severe black suit, sharp white shirt and burgundy tie, Nathan Wolfe was a mind-boggling, lust-inducing sight.

They simply stood there staring at each other.

"Yes," Mariah said with satisfaction.

"Oh, my yes," Sierra agreed.

Nathan turned his glare on his smug sisters-in-law. "What are you trying to do to me?"

They grinned.

Then the door opened, and Dominic stuck his head in. "Car's waiting. Let's go."

Carin felt a shaft of pure panic, now that the moment had arrived. She was actually grateful when Nathan's hand closed around hers.

He gave her a wink and a grin. "Stick with me. You'll be fine. I'll take care of everything."

In fact he did. She didn't want to admit it, but by deflecting some of the attention and answering nosey questions with exactly the right mixture of nonsense, jargon and charm, Nathan made the whole experience far less of an ordeal than it would have been without his presence.

People—especially women—gravitated to him, talked to him, demanded his attention. And he gave it to them, but at the same time he kept a hand on Carin. He drew her into the conversation, introduced her to everyone, made sure they knew this was *her* show, not his.

"It's sort of a family affair," he said when they asked why his photos were being displayed with hers. "Some of our daughter's work is here, too."

Lacey had been amazed at the sight of her own work hung with her parents'. "I took that picture," she whispered to her grandfather when she caught sight of the first one—a shot of Zeno and Miss Saffron's cat, momentarily friends, curled up together in the shade of a palm.

She walked around the gallery wide-eyed, grinning from ear to ear. And when she found Carin and Nathan, she hugged them both, and Carin thought she saw tears in her daughter's eyes. More than once that night, watching Lacey, watching Nathan and his family—feeling the connections between them and wishing—Carin had felt tears of her own.

It would be so wonderful to be a part of this family. A real part. A beloved part—not just a duty.

"Lovely show." A woman's voice called her back to the present, and she turned to see Gabriela, Nathan's agent, smiling at her. "Looks like it all worked out."

Carin nodded. "Thanks to Nathan." She didn't hesitate to admit that.

"Oh, Nathan's a brick," Gabriela said dryly, then she turned to him. "I need to talk with you."

Nathan frowned. "Now?"

"Now. Sorry." She gave Carin a commiserating smile. "I'll return him in a moment. We have a bit of business. Then I have to catch a plane back to Santa Fe."

"Of course." Carin smiled at her. "I can manage," she assured Nathan, who looked as if he were going to argue with Gabriela.

Nathan's jaw worked for a moment. He hesitated, then shrugged. "Okay. One minute." He took Gabriela's arm and they moved to a corner of the room where Carin tried not to watch them talking. But whether she wanted to or not, her gaze kept drifting their way.

Gabriela was apparently determined to make the most of her minute. She was talking nonstop, gesturing, pointing, obviously feeling very strongly about something.

Nathan was leaning against the wall, hands tucked in his pockets, looking casual. But from the way his jaw tightened as he listened to her words, he didn't seem to be as non-chalant as his pose might suggest.

They were too far away for Carin to have any idea what they were saying. It wasn't her business anyway, she told herself severely. And she was glad when Stacia brought over a journalist to talk with her.

Carin mustered her own charm and wits and tried to an-swer his questions. All the while, though, her gaze went back to Nathan and Gaby. Gaby had her hand on his sleeve now, gesturing expansively with her other hand toward his photos, then spreading her palms and giving him an irri-tated look which wasn't hard to read.

And where are the rest of them? she seemed to ask.

Nathan's shoulders hunched. His spine stiffened. He said something, then shook his head fiercely.

Whatever he said, Gaby didn't agree with. That was ob-vious from her stance, from her stiff shoulders, from her waggling finger under his nose.

Nathan shoved her finger away and, clearly annoyed, pushed away from the wall and dipped his head toward where Lacey was standing with Mariah and Rhys. Then his gaze flickered briefly in Carin's direction. Gabriela's gaze followed his. She shook her head, then began arguing again. She looked annoyed, too, now. Whatever point she'd tried to make, Nathan had rejected.

He shook his head, then turned and walked away, leaving her alone as he headed back toward Carin.

Determinedly Gaby followed. "You're going to regret it, Nathan. It's a terrific opportunity."

Nathan ignored her. A muscle was ticking in his jaw. "You okay?" he asked Carin, as if she were the one under attack at the moment.

"Fine."

"See. She's fine," Gaby said. "She'd want—" Gaby began.

Nathan whirled on her. "Don't," he said fiercely. "Don't involve her."

Gaby's mouth was open. The words—whatever they were—were on the tip of her tongue. Carin could almost hear them. But Nathan had made his own point.

Gaby pressed her lips into a firm line. Her expression grew shuttered, and she turned to look at Nathan. "You're making it hard to be your agent."

He scowled. "So quit."

"I don't want to quit," Gaby said patiently. "I love your work. I love what you've done, what you *could* do!"

Nathan let out a harsh impatient breath. He shot back his cuff and looked at his watch. "You'll miss your plane, Gaby."

"Think about it."

"I've told you—"

"Think about it. And call me when you get back to the Bahamas." She smiled suddenly, then leaned forward and gave him a quick kiss. Then she turned her gaze on Carin. "It's been a great show," she said. "You two work well together." Her gaze flicked back to Nathan. "But there's only so much you can do on an island. *You* need to get back to work, Nathan."

And then with a waggling wave of her fingers, she was gone.

"Where does she want you to go?" Carin asked.

"Doesn't matter. I'm not going." He didn't even look at her. He was scanning the crowd. "There's Finn MacCauley and his wife. Finn's a terrific photographer—and a good friend of Rhys's. Come on. I'll introduce you."

And that was the end of whatever Gaby had in mind.

Finn MacCauley and his wife Izzy had a pair of twins who were just a bit younger than Lacey. Izzy promptly invited Lacey over to meet them the following afternoon.

"We're only here one more day," Carin said. "I thought we'd go somewhere."

"Drop her off," Izzy said. "You and Nathan go somewhere."

"We don't need—"

"Of course you do. Every couple with kids needs time alone together," Izzy said flatly. "I know. We have four. And when you come to pick her up we'll have a barbecue. I'll invite Gib and Chloe—they're here somewhere." She stood on tiptoe, looking around, and not seeing them, shrugged. "And Sam and Josie. They're in the city for a week. It'll be fun."

Steamrollered, all Carin could do was ask, "Who are Gib and Chloe and Sam and Josie?"

"Gib's a photographer. Finn's competition," Izzy added dryly. "He and Finn are always one-upping each other." Izzy laughed. "They're actually best friends, but the rivalry seems to spur them to greater achievements. And Sam's my ex-fiancé. Josie's his wife."

Carin blinked. She could just about swallow the "best friends/competitors" notion. But her mind balked at Izzy so cavalierly inviting her ex-fiancé to come to a barbecue. Something of her astonishment must have been evident on her face because Izzy laughed.

"We're good friends, Sam and I. We were *always* good friends. Unlike Finn and I." She shot a wry—and adoring—look at her husband who was deep in conversation with Nathan. Then she put a hand on Carin's arm. "Finn says I simply push people, and you don't have to agree. But it would be fun for the girls to meet Lacey. And who knows, maybe we'll get to the Bahamas again. Finn goes on shoots all over. Maybe sometime the kids and I could come.''

"That would be fun," Carin agreed. She didn't want Izzy MacCauley to think her unfriendly. "And as for tomorrow, I—I'll talk to Nathan."

She didn't really want to be "alone together" with Nathan at all. But she did want to know what Gaby had talked to him about. Was Gaby pressuring him to take an assignment? It seemed likely.

Despite what he'd said about staying on Pelican Cay, they all knew he couldn't stay forever.

But there was no time to pursue the matter further. Not that night. They fell into bed exhausted as soon as they got home.

In the morning Douglas took all of them out to brunch to celebrate the success of the opening. He made a point of seating himself between Carin and Lacey, talking with Carin about her work, about her plans for the shop, about what she'd like to do next, and talking to Lacey about her photography.

That some of her photos had been in the show last night had delighted Lacey. But clearly what delighted her more was having a grandfather who doted on her, having uncles who teased her, an aunt who braided her hair, cousins who followed her around like ducklings.

Lacey was blossoming. She'd always been an outgoing child, but sometimes Carin thought Lacey tried too hard, displaying an almost overeager need to belong to whatever group she was in. Perhaps because she wasn't sure she did belong?

Carin hadn't considered that before. She didn't like considering it now.

Except she could see a difference here. With Douglas and his sons and their families, Lacey did belong. There was acceptance. No need to prove herself. She was part of this family.

Douglas turned his attention from his granddaughter to Nathan. "Heading back for the island now?"

"Yes."

"Still working on the book?"

Nathan nodded.

"So," Douglas said eagerly, "what's next?"

"Dunno." Nathan didn't look as if he cared, either. He cut another piece of pancake and swabbed it in the syrup on his plate.

Douglas looked surprised. He tapped his fingers on the table impatiently. "Surely you must have something lined up."

"Not at the moment." Nathan turned away from his father, looking at Rhys instead. "How about you and Mariah bringing the kids down this fall?"

"Yeah, sure. If you're going to be there."

"I'm going to be there," Nathan said almost fiercely.

Both Douglas and Rhys looked at him, surprised.

The subject of Nathan's work wasn't brought up again. It didn't stop Carin from thinking about it. And when Izzy called shortly after they got back to Mariah's and suggested coming by to pick Lacey up, Carin found herself saying yes.

As soon as Lacey left with the MacCauleys, Carin went in search of Nathan.

He was standing on the deck of their little studio apartment. He had his hands braced on the railing and was staring out over the gardens. But as she stood inside the screen door and watched him, she didn't think he was seeing any of them. His mind seemed a thousand miles away.

"Lacey left with Izzy," Carin said, opening the screen door.

Nathan whirled around, his expression betraying his surprise at the sight of her. Whatever else was going on in his head, though, she couldn't tell.

"They invited us to a barbecue at their place later to-night," she went on. "They're very nice."

"Yeah, they are."

She put her hands on the back of one of the deck chairs. It gave her something to hold on to. "Did Gaby have an offer for you?"

"What?" He scowled, then raked a hand through his hair. Shrugging, he turned away. "She's always got ideas."

"She thinks you need to get back to work."

He turned his head and glared at her. "I've been work-ing."

"Yes." She moved around the chair and went to stand alongside him, looking out over the tiny back gardens two stories below. "But you can't do that forever. What is Gaby's idea?"

"Another book about Zeno. The publisher wants me to go back, follow him some more. See if he's still out there. Shoot the sequel." Nathan's mouth twisted.

"That's a wonderful idea."

"Just dandy. But I'm not going."

"Why not? Lacey would be so impressed."

Nathan's knuckles whitened on the railing. He didn't say anything. He didn't look at her now. He stared out into the gardens.

"You don't have to stay just because you told me you were going to," Carin went on carefully in the face of his silence.

"Yes, I do," he said through his teeth. "I'm going to stay."

"Why?"

"Because," he said, turning now so that his blue gaze collided with hers, "I'm not leaving until you marry me. I told you that."

"But it's a good idea. And you can't—"

His jaw clenched. "I'm not going, Carin. You're not getting rid of me that way." He turned away and strode quickly back into the apartment. He banged out the door and clattered down the stairs without a backward glance.

The summer night was warm but not humid. The backyard barbecue at the MacCauleys was a resounding success.

Lacey and Finn and Izzy's daughters—"They used to be nieces," Lacey informed Carin, "but Finn and Izzy adopted them"—had become fast friends. They shared interests in photography and painting and a boy band that had a cute lead singer. Lacey was eager for them to come visit at Pelican Cay. And not just Tansy and Pansy, the twins, but Finn and Izzy and the little boys, too.

She thought the little boys, Rip and Crash—"Don't ask," said Izzy when she introduced Carin to the two dark-haired preschoolers—were so much fun.

"I wouldn't mind a brother," Lacey confided to Carin, "now that Dad's back."

The look Carin gave her must have precipitated second thoughts because Lacey said quickly, "Or, um, not." And seeing Izzy carrying a tray of lemonade out onto the patio, she hurried to help, leaving her mother by herself—to observe, to ponder, to reflect.

It was a lovely evening. A good time was had by all. And it was nearly eleven by the time they all got back to Rhys and Mariah's. Stephen and Lizzie fell asleep in the stroller. Lacey, who had bounced through the evening, began to slow down on the walk back uptown.

They had to get up early to catch a flight and so, when they got home, she fell into bed without a murmur and only one question.

"We can come back soon, can't we, Mom?"

Carin smiled and kissed her good-night. Then she took a shower while Nathan made up the beds. When she came out, the beds were made up, and he said gruffly, "My turn," and brushed past her into the bathroom.

Carin lay down on the bed and stared at the ceiling.

When she'd imagined coming to New York with Lacey, it hadn't been to a place like this. She'd imagined a hotel, not a home. She'd imagined strangers, not friends. She'd imagined herself and Lacey on their own.

It hadn't been anything like that.

But it had been good.

Even in her sleep, Lacey had had a smile on her face. She'd had a wonderful time in New York. She'd had a wonderful time with her family. With the Wolfes. She loved them, and they clearly loved her. They'd taken her into their hearts and their homes.

They had done much the same with Carin. Though Dominic had reason to dislike her, though they all had reason to resent her for what she'd done to Dominic and then for having kept Lacey's existence hidden for so long, they had actually welcomed her, too.

They had made her feel as if she was a part of their family. They had rekindled her longings, had reanimated her dreams. They had made her want things she had long ago told herself she would never have—not with Nathan.

The shower shut off. She heard him moving around in the bathroom. Seconds later the door opened and he appeared, lean and hard and beautiful, wearing only boxers, as he moved toward his bed.

She wanted him. Still. All the years and all the determination and all the heartache never managed to change that.

But what about Nathan? What did Nathan want? Really?

He pushed back the sheet and slid in, lying down flat on his back. If Carin looked at him out of the corner of her eye, she could see the rise and fall of his chest.

She knew what he would say he wanted—her. But that was duty speaking. And she didn't want him to marry her because of "duty". But she knew he wasn't going to turn his back on that duty. Obviously, he would turn his back on his career first.

In the silence she drew a breath. "Nathan?"

He jumped at the sound of her voice, then let out a harsh sigh, as if he'd hoped she was asleep and had suddenly discovered she was not. "What?"

She swallowed and stared at the ceiling, afraid to look at him, knowing her own duty. "I'm ready to get married."

CHAPTER TEN

NATHAN ROLLED onto his side and stared at her, unsure he'd heard right.

Carin didn't stare back. She didn't even look at him. She was staring straight at the ceiling, looking like one of those bodies carved on the tops of sarcophagi, hands folded below her breasts, eyes focused on the heavens.

He ran his tongue over his lips. "You're ready to get married?" He cleared his throat. "To who?"

Her head whipped around and she rolled to face him. Even in the near darkness he could see the outraged expression on her face. "Fine! Never mind. I just thought it made sense, but if you don't want to, that's perfectly okay with me." There was a high, tight tone in her voice that surprised him.

He held up a hand. "Whoa! Hang on. You just... surprised me. You're serious?"

"No, I'm joking. Of course, I'm serious."

"Why? Why now?" More to the point.

For that he got another glare. But damn it, he needed to ask. Dared to hope.

Carin pressed her lips together for a long moment, then she gave a little shrug. "It makes sense." She didn't sound annoyed now. She sounded distant, almost indifferent.

Nathan's hopes wavered. Hardly a declaration of her undying love. "Sense?"

She gave him an impatient scowl. "You're the one who thought so in the first place. Duty and responsibility and all that. Isn't that what you said?"

"Yeah, but—"

"Well, I've decided you're right. You're not the only one who can be dutiful and responsible." Her chin jutted.

Nathan felt a hollow ache begin. "So," he said slowly, "you're willing to get married out of duty?"

"Yes. It would be good for Lacey."

"I said that weeks ago."

"With just us, I couldn't see it. But now that I've seen her with your brothers and your father and your family...she's happy. I mean, she was happy before, but she didn't have a family. Lacey always wanted a family." The tightness was there in her voice again. Nathan wasn't sure what it meant.

So it all came back to Lacey?

"And that's all?" He shouldn't push. He couldn't make her say words that weren't true—even if he wanted desperately to hear them.

"I figure it's better for you, too. So you can go back to work. Do the assignment Gabriela wants you to do."

His teeth came together. "*That's* why you're marrying me? To get rid of me?"

"I'm trying to be sensible, Nathan. You'll hurt your career by insisting on staying, by being so stubborn. And if you don't know it, I do. I'm trying to tell you don't have to."

"Thanks very much," he said bitterly.

"Look," Carin said impatiently, "you wanted us to be a family. You came down insisting that I marry you so you could 'do the right thing'. Fine, I've agreed. Let's do it. We'll get married—and then you can get back to your life!"

His life. He didn't have a life anymore—not without Carin and Lacey.

But how the hell could he say that when she was wishing him gone? And how the hell could he pack up and leave without marrying her if she was finally agreeable?

It might be a marriage built on duty, but at least it would be a marriage—a starting point.

Given time, Nathan told himself, they could build something solid. They could find the love they'd lost—the love he'd killed. And yes, he might have to go away from time to time, but perhaps they would go with him. He'd have a right to ask them to if he and Carin were married. And even if she said no, if they were married he would always have the right to come back.

So he didn't get love in the bargain. At least he got the chance to earn it.

"Okay," he said. "Let's do it."

They did it.

Early the next morning Nathan canceled their flight home. "Got other plans," he told Rhys who was fixing toast fingers for Stephen. "We'll go tomorrow. Today we're getting married."

Rhys's jaw dropped. The knife clattered to the floor.

Nathan glared. "Don't act surprised. It's what everybody wanted."

"Well, yeah," Rhys said, then added carefully, "As long as it's what you want."

"It's what I want. Can Dominic pull some strings? Get us a license and a J.P.?"

"He did it for himself," Rhys said. "I don't see why he wouldn't do it for you." He paused. "Does Carin know about this?"

"Of course she knows. It was her damned idea!"

Rhys raised a brow. "And is she as happy about it as you are?"

"I don't think so, no," Nathan said honestly. He punched in Dominic's phone number. "Hey," he said when his brother answered. "Is this Weddings by Wolfe? Want to be my best man?"

Dominic, thank God, was enthusiastic. He didn't ask annoying questions like Rhys did. He said, "I'll take care of everything and call you back."

He called back in less than an hour with everything arranged. "Everything but a dress," he said. "Sierra said she and Mariah can help Carin with that." He rattled off an address downtown. "Be there by three-thirty." He paused. "Is Carin cool with this?"

"Why does everybody think I'm forcing her to marry me?"

"Just wondered. Anyway, speaking from experience," Dominic said dryly, "I'm sure if she doesn't want to, she just won't show up."

Lacey was thrilled when Carin told her the news. She gasped, grinned, then whooped and yelled and threw her arms around her mother.

"I knew it! I knew you still loved each other! Oh, this is perfect! Wait'll I tell Tansy and Pansy. Wait'll I tell Lorenzo." She jumped out of bed and began dancing around the room.

Carin took comfort in the fact that Lacey was delighted, because for her part, she was scared to death about what she'd done.

She'd caved in.

She'd rationalized it to Nathan—she'd babbled on about wanting Lacey to have a solid connection to her uncles and grandfather, about Lacey herself wanting to be part of a family. She'd brought up Nathan's career and what he owed to it.

All very true.

But she never said the truest thing of all—that she was marrying Nathan because she loved him, because she wanted to spend the rest of her life with him. And she simply couldn't fight it any longer. She could deny him the words because she didn't want to be pathetic, because she didn't want him feeling sorry for her.

But she couldn't deny it in her heart.

She had sworn she wouldn't marry unless her love was reciprocated. But that was selfish—and it was asking for the impossible. You couldn't make a person love you.

She wished Nathan loved her, but right now she would take what she could get. She was too weak to fight any longer.

It was the right thing to do for Lacey. It was the right thing to do for Nathan.

And if she knew the pain of loving without being loved—well, it couldn't be helped. At least she would have him in her life.

Maybe, given time…

But she wouldn't let herself go there.

First she would marry him. Then she would hope he would fall in love with her.

"You're *married*?" Fiona was astonished to hear the news.

"You got hitched?" Hugh didn't sound quite so surprised.

"'Bout time, that's what I say." Estelle put her hands on her hips and gave them a satisfied smile. "Didn't I tell you they were right for each other?" she asked her husband, Maurice.

Maurice bobbed his head. "You surely did."

"Well, if you're all done passing judgment," Nathan said, "maybe you could give me a hand putting the luggage in the Jeep. Carin and Lacey brought back presents for everyone on the island."

It was a calculated request, meant to make clear—in case Carin or Hugh or anyone else had other ideas—that Carin and Lacey were coming home with him. He shouldn't have had to worry.

But though she had smiled at the wedding and though she had let him hold her hand during the reception and put his arm around her when they left Rhys and Mariah's a day late, she had never unbent.

She hadn't bolted as she had when she'd been going to marry Dominic. She had shown up. She had said her vows. But the woman who had married him yesterday was definitely a woman fulfilling a duty. He had his work cut out for him.

"Can Zeno come?" Lacey asked.

Since Zeno had already jumped in the Jeep, and was even now panting happily at Nathan, there was only one answer. Nathan was inclined to say yes, anyway. "Sure. Why not?"

Lacey talked all the way home, making plans for tomorrow, who to go see, who to tell about her adventures, who to regale with the story of her parents' wedding.

Nathan let it all wash over him, making appropriate noises when required. It went with being a father, he'd discovered. He had no problem with it. So far fatherhood had come remarkably easily.

It was being a husband that was going to be tricky.

He wanted to be a good one. He wanted to be a real one.

So when Carin opened her mouth as he carried the bags upstairs, he said flatly, "We're married. We're sharing a bedroom."

Carin's expression grew shuttered and unreadable. But she closed her mouth and gave an almost imperceptible nod of her head.

So much for romance.

Of course she didn't expect it. She'd warned herself not to. They were married, but it was hardly a marriage of love.

Still, somehow she had hoped.

Fool, Carin derided herself. *You knew better.* But even so, it hurt that he was so abrupt, so harsh. He wanted her physically, that much was clear. He would share his body with her. But he wasn't going to give her his heart.

She wished she could refuse to sleep with him. She couldn't. Lacey would expect them to sleep together. But even acknowledging that, Carin knew it wasn't the whole truth—the truth was she wanted him. It was pathetic. *She* was pathetic.

But if this marriage was not going to be complete misery, they had to start somewhere.

They might as well start in bed. It was the place their relationship had begun to go wrong. Maybe now they could start to put it right.

They managed to be pleasant and polite, even teasing a bit, while Lacey was still up. But as soon as she'd gone to bed, the tension between them grew like a storm filling the sky. It wasn't terribly late, but all Carin could think about was her bag upstairs in Nathan's bedroom, about what it meant, about what the night would bring.

"Do you want a glass of wine?" Nathan asked. She was standing on the deck, staring out at the ocean, hoping that the evening breeze would cool her heated flesh.

Quickly she shook her head. "I'm fine. I...think I might like a bath."

When she'd finished she put on a thin silk nightgown— a gift from Mariah and Sierra and far more elegant than the T-shirt and gym shorts she'd worn in New York—and went into the bedroom.

Nathan was already there. He took one look at her, and something flared in his gaze. His jaw tightened and his whole body seemed to grow taut.

He'd already begun to undress. His shirt was unbuttoned, hanging loose and affording her a glimpse of his hard muscled chest. The glimpse only made her want more. She remembered the night she'd seen him coming up from the sea, remembered the sight of his naked body, and her breath caught and her pulse quickened as she anticipated seeing it again.

Nathan, hearing the catch of her breath, scowled. "Don't go all innocent virgin on me," he said, misinterpreting it.

"No fear," Carin retorted sharply, annoyed. "You already took care of that."

They glared at each other, electricity arcing between them.

"I damned well never forced you."

Carin's gaze slid away. "I know that," she muttered.

"And I don't want to force you now." Then he let his shirt fall to the floor and crossed the room to her. He put his hands on her arms, slid them down, then touched her waist, drew her close. His breath stirred tendrils of her hair. His stubbled jaw scraped lightly against her own.

And Carin trembled.

Nathan stilled, then stepped back. "Are you afraid of me?"

She shook her head resolutely. "N-no." It wasn't Nathan she was afraid of. It was her own traitorous heart.

"Then love me," Nathan said hoarsely. "Let me love you." And he drew her to the bed, and they lay down upon it.

Together, where they had longed to be, their bodies seemed unable to resist. Their limbs tangled, their mouths met, their tongues clashed. Carin felt his hands on her, stroking and teasing her breasts, her belly, her legs, the very center of her, finding her wet and waiting, making her writhe.

Determined to have her own way, Carin touched him, too. Her fingers sought his belt and unfastened it, tugged the zip and pulled it down. She pushed his khakis and boxers down his hips and, willingly, he kicked them away. Then he shoved her gown up and yanked it over her head and they faced each other, naked and hungry, eyes glittering, passions flaming.

It had been so long. So very very long. And yet, right

now, right this very moment, Carin knew that whatever had kept them apart, in this at least nothing had changed.

"Carin?"

She trembled, nodded. "Nathan."

And then he was kissing her and she was kissing him. He pressed her back onto the bed and slipped between her legs. He touched the liquid core of her and made her shiver, made her body open. And Carin touched the hard, hot length of his erection, ran her fingers over him lightly, saw him bite his lip and shut his eyes, felt him shudder and tense.

And then she drew him in.

It was a heat and a fullness she had never forgotten. It was a melding of bodies, a connection between souls. She had thought that once. She prayed it would happen again.

Love me, Nathan had said. *Let me love you.*

And as they began to move together, as their rhythms meshed and their bodies became one, Carin felt tears prick her eyelids as she prayed that he meant more than the pleasure their bodies were taking in each other.

He'd said her name. He'd asked. She'd answered.

It was a start.

If only he loved her and would let her love him…life would be beautiful.

It was a truce, Nathan supposed. A marriage built on duty and their daughter.

It was what he had asked for—and what he had got.

They were a family of sorts. They lived at Nathan's, all three of them and Zeno the dog. And during the days they settled into a routine. Lacey went to school, Nathan worked on his book, and Carin, once she got her arm out of the cast, went back to working in the shop and started painting again.

They were polite to each other—maybe more than polite. They smiled, they talked, and sometimes, tentatively, they teased. They were moving in the right direction, building connections.

But Nathan wanted so much more.

He wanted the casual contact he'd seen between Dominic and Sierra, between Rhys and Mariah. He wanted to be able to come up behind Carin while she was doing the dishes or working in the shop and slide his arms around her and pull her back against him and kiss the nape of her neck. He wanted to take her hand when they walked along the beach. He wanted to tell her that he loved her.

But he was afraid to push. He'd got this far, he told himself. He had her in his home. At night he had her in his bed. It was the one time that their inhibitions seemed to vanish. Their limbs tangled, their bodies merged. Physically they connected.

But they never spoke endearments. They never talked of love.

Someday they would, he told himself. But he had no idea when.

When Gaby called the first time, he said no. He wasn't ready. He was still on his honeymoon, he told her.

"It's been a month," Gaby said.

"I'm not ready," Nathan told her.

She called again a week later. And a week after that. He stalled her. Hedged. Put it off. Yes, he wanted to do what she wanted him to do—spend three months in the wilderness checking out the wolf Zeno or, if that didn't work, then a project of his own choosing.

He wanted to do it—but he wanted his marriage on solid ground first. Even better, he wanted Carin and Lacey to come with him. But he couldn't say so.

Gaby said it for him. "If you want to bring Carin and Lacey, do it," she'd said.

"I...can't," Nathan said awkwardly. "School, you know. And Carin's got her painting. Her business."

"She can get a lot of new material if she comes with you," Gaby said. "And think how educational it would be for Lacey."

"Mmm." Yes. Yes to all of the above. But he still couldn't ask.

He was afraid to. Afraid Carin would say no. Afraid he'd lose whatever advances he'd made over the past two months. Afraid if he left she would rejoice in his going and he would know she didn't love him—not really.

Afraid she wouldn't want him to come back.

"Well," Gaby said impatiently when he didn't answer.

"I'll think about it."

He thought about nothing else. He rehearsed a hundred ways to ask Carin—and Lacey—to come with him.

You could paint the north woods. You could paint wolves. Lacey would learn so much. Think of the educational opportunities. Not many kids ever get a chance to do something like that. I could show you my world. We could share it.

But that was getting dangerously close to personal. It was almost like saying *I love you,* and Nathan couldn't do that because he was afraid she didn't love him.

If he knew she did, it would be easy. If only he could figure that out without having to ask. He needed a sign, he thought, as he walked up to the house with Lacey three nights later, Zeno bouncing along ahead, darting after a lizard here and a frog there.

They had been out shooting in the twilight, and Nathan had talked a little about the light in the north woods. If Lacey said, "When are you going again?" he thought he would mention Gaby's offer.

But Lacey didn't ask. It didn't seem to occur to her that he would have to go again. Because he'd said he would stay forever, he reminded himself. Or take them with him.

Carin was in the kitchen when they came onto the deck. "Wash your hands. Supper's ready," she said. She didn't smile the way she usually did when they got home. She wasn't frowning exactly. She just seemed...remote.

"Something wrong?" Nathan asked.

"Wrong?" Blonde brows lifted. "What could be wrong?"

He didn't know. Still he felt an odd clutching in his gut at her words. A premonition?

He found out that night when they were going to bed.

"Gaby called," Carin said. She was brushing out her hair and she didn't turn around. But he could see her face in the mirror.

Nathan went very still. "Did she? What did she say?"

"She wanted to know what you'd decided about going up north." Carin's words were flat.

Nathan scrubbed a hand over his hair. The moment of truth. *Smile at me, damn it. Give me some encouragement,* he begged her.

But Carin just kept on brushing her hair. She didn't even look at him.

He paced around their bedroom. "I know I said I'd stay forever," he began.

"And we both know that's impossible," Carin said sharply.

"Well, I—"

"Gaby told me you need to go." Carin's tone was firm.

"I—" Hell. How could he just blurt out an invitation now? Damn Gaby, anyway! "I'll be back."

Carin's mouth pressed into a thin line. Her expression grew shuttered. "Lacey will be glad to know that," she said dully. Their eyes met in the mirror. And then her gaze dropped.

Nathan sighed. "I'll call Gaby in the morning."

"Good idea." Carin set the brush down, then got up and crossed the room. She slipped into bed and pulled the covers up.

Nathan shut off the light and came to slide in beside her.

Every night since their marriage they'd touched, they'd made love or they just wrapped their arms around each other and slept.

Tonight they lay inches apart. But neither reached across those few inches.

"Good night, Nathan," Carin said tonelessly. Then she rolled onto her side, turning away.

They went through the next three days like zombies. Polite, civil zombies who shared a bed and a daughter—and nothing else.

The rapport they'd built over the past weeks had vanished just as Nathan had feared it would. Carin shut him out and retreated into a shell. So much for wanting to take her with him.

Her indifference now was killing him. If he was going, he had to go now!

He called Gaby and told her, "Get me on the first flight you can."

She'd called last night. "Get to Miami in the morning. Your flight leaves at one."

Hugh agreed to take him. He had a cargo that needed to be delivered. "If you don't mind the seaplane," he said.

"Anything."

Even so, saying goodbye to his daughter nearly did him in. Lacey was distraught to learn that he was going away. She'd been sulking since he'd told her. "You could take us," she'd said.

But Nathan, seeing Carin's back stiffen at her words, had said, "No, I can't." He didn't say he wished he could.

Now Lacey wrapped her arms around him and gave him a fierce hug. "You'd better come back."

"Of course I will. Soon." It was the best he could do.

"You'll e-mail? You'll call?"

"Yes. And you will, too?"

"Of course," she said indignantly. "I love you."

Nathan's mouth twisted at the ease with which she spoke such words. He pressed his lips to the top of her head and held her close. "Likewise, kiddo."

"I'll come to the harbor to see you leave," she said.

"No, you won't," Carin said firmly. "You have to get to school."

"But—"

Carin looked at Nathan expectantly. He knew what she was waiting for.

"Go to school, Lace," he said heavily.

Their daughter sighed. She gave him one more fierce hug, then reluctantly she got on her bike and wobbled off down the road.

Then it was just him and Carin—and Carin wouldn't even look at him. She started cleaning the table, turning her back on him, washing up the breakfast dishes.

"Carin?" He came up behind her. One last chance. *Tell me you'll miss me. Tell me you love me.*

"Don't let me keep you," she said, and stepped away abruptly when he would have kissed her goodbye.

And just like that, he was gone.

There was a moment's hesitation when Carin thought he might have insisted on that kiss, when—God help her!— she wished he would.

But then wordlessly he'd turned, picked up his bag and walked out the door.

And there was none of the relief Carin had promised herself she would feel seeing him go. None of the satisfaction of knowing she'd been the one to turn away from him, that she had not let him have things his way, that she had never given in.

Instead she felt hollow, aching, desperate. It wasn't supposed to be like this!

She stood, rigid, soaked in pain and loneliness, and knew

the truth at last—that in denying him, she'd denied herself, as well.

She loved Nathan Wolfe. She would always love him.

And not admitting it didn't mean it wasn't so.

Not admitting it meant she was a coward, that she was afraid to take a risk. She'd refused to let herself hope. She'd tried every way she could to protect her heart, to deny her love. But it wasn't possible.

And it didn't hurt less for trying. If anything it hurt more.

She could have wrapped her arms around him. She could have held him. She could have had his kiss to remember, to savor. She could have said, "I love you."

And maybe…just maybe…he would have said it back.

Maybe it wasn't too late. If she could get to the harbor before they took off. She grabbed her tote bag and started to run.

She was almost to the village when she saw Hugh's seaplane circle above the bay.

She stopped, heart aching, and watched it go.

She made it to the shop before the tears began to fall. She sniffled and swiped at them, worried that someone would come in and see her. Please God, for a while at least, the tourists would stay well away.

But even as she thought the words, the door banged open.

She blew her nose, scrubbed at her eyes and pasted on a smile. "May I help— Estelle? What's wrong?"

"It's Nathan! Come quick." The whites of Estelle's eyes were enormous in her dark face. She turned and ran back out again.

Carin's bones turned to water. Her knees wobbled. Bile rose in her throat. Nathan! Ohmigod, Nathan! And Hugh, of course. But— *Nathan*!!!!

She ran after Estelle, out the door and down the steps, tripping, stumbling. "What happened? Did they crash?"

"Yes," Estelle said. "Yes!"

In the harbor? Were they still alive? Being rescued? Carin couldn't ask, could only run.

And then she saw him—limping up the road.

Limping up the road?

Carin stared. In the *road*? Not in the *harbor*?

But yes, it was Nathan, not fifty yards from her, with Estelle bearing down on him. She fluttered at him, but he brushed her off and soldiered on, scraped and battered, one arm looking wonky, an abrasion on his cheek—but *alive!*—and heading straight toward her.

Where was the plane? Where was Hugh? What in the world—?

They met in the middle of Pineapple Street, stopped an arm's length apart and stared at each other. Carin wanted to grab him and hold him, but could only shake her head.

"What—" she began.

"The plane?" she tried.

"You crashed?" she guessed.

"It was that bloody dog," Nathan said gruffly.

"The dog? *Zeno*?" Carin stared, astonished. Something dangerously close to a hysterical laugh threatened to bubble up. But it wasn't funny at all and yet—

"Zeno," Nathan confirmed, through gritted teeth.

Estelle was flapping at him, yammering about doctors and hospitals. They both ignored her.

"I thought…" Carin began. Her teeth beginning to chatter. It was shock, she thought. And joy. Pure joy at the sight of him. "What are you…? Didn't Hugh wait for you?"

She couldn't imagine Hugh leaving without him. Of course he had cargo, but surely he'd have waited if Nathan had been late. But Nathan hadn't been late. Had he?

"You better get yourself over to Doc Rasmussen's right now," Estelle said.

"Later," Nathan said firmly to Estelle. "Go away."

There was something in his tone that stopped all the flut-

tering and the yammering. Estelle looked at him, at the way
he was looking only at Carin, then slowly she smiled and
nodded her head. "I tell the doc you be along."

"Do that," Nathan said without glancing her way. He
had eyes only for Carin. "I told Hugh to go without me."

"Because Zeno—"

"Zeno got me on my way back."

Carin stared. "What?"

"I didn't go with Hugh. I told him I wasn't ready. He
brought me back to shore and I borrowed a bike. I was in
a hurry. So was Zeno," he said dryly.

"But...but why?"

"Because I love you."

She stared at him. Words she'd almost given up hope
on, words she'd feared never to hear were right there before
her. More than that, though, there was the way Nathan was
looking at her, intent, determined, and with a light in his
eyes that she was sure met a matching one in her own.

Her jaw wobbled. Her eyes filled. "Oh, God, Nathan!"

"Don't cry, for heaven's sake!" he begged her, distraught. "I'm sorry. If you don't want to hear it, I'm sorry!
I couldn't leave without saying—"

"I *want* to hear it!" She would have flung her arms
around him if she could have figured out how to do it
without hurting him. "I love you! I love you, too!"

And then he wrapped his one good arm around her. And
right there in the middle of Pineapple Street, right in front
of the Win Pixie grocery store and the Pelican Cay school,
Nathan was kissing her, hungrily, desperately.

And despite her fear of hurting him further, Carin was
kissing him back.

"I love you," she said again. Her voice broke, but her
spirit soared. The words, once spoken, were now easy to
say. She smiled against his lips, tears threatening again. She
dashed them away. "I ran after you to tell you. I didn't

want you to go without knowing. I thought you'd gone.... And then I thought the plane..."

She started to cry in earnest now. And Nathan was hanging on to her, shaking his head. "Not gone. Not going. Not without you. I couldn't."

There were kids gathering at the windows of the school, watching, grinning. "Hey, Lace! Lookit! It's your mom and dad. They're kissin'."

But Carin barely heard them. She only looked at Nathan. "But you have to go. It's what you do. I don't expect you to stay for us."

"I'll go again," Nathan told her. He looked down at his arm which was probably broken and hurt like hell—but not as much as going without them had. "But only if you and Lacey come with me."

"Of course." Carin smiled up at him through her tears. "Of course we will."

Was it that simple? Nathan wondered, dazed. Would he wake up in Doc Rasmussen's and discover he'd dreamed it all.

But then Lacey was there, and all her classmates, whooping and cheering.

"We have to get you to the doctor," Carin said, easing an arm around his waist, trying to get him to walk with her.

"In a sec," Nathan said, reveling in the moment. He wasn't dreaming. There was no way he could have dreamed up an elementary school full of cheering kids. He kissed her again, and she kissed him back willingly. He needed this far more than he needed a doctor or X-rays or Band-Aids.

He needed Carin—and Lacey—more than he needed anything else on earth.

"Come on, Nathan," Carin urged him. "We need to get you to the doc and then home to bed."

"Bed?" Nathan said hopefully.

Carin looked up into his eyes and he looked down into hers. They looked at each other tenderly, laughingly, lovingly. "Oh, definitely," Carin said.

And then together, with her supporting him, they limped off up the street.

Zeno watched them, then looked at Lacey and wagged his tail.

Not bad, his eyes said, for a morning's work.

New York City, One Year Later

This time it was Nathan's show.

They all had a part again this year—Nathan, Carin and Lacey. It made sense, Gaby agreed, because they'd all gone on the expedition together. It had been a family affair.

With Nathan's arm broken and winter fast closing in, they couldn't leave until spring. But in May the three of them had flown up into the north woods. The temperatures had still been just south of frigid. The snow had been thick on the ground. It had been an education for Lacey, all right.

It had been a time to remember for all of them.

Now they were sharing the memories with the world at large. The book, *Not So Solo*, would be published just before Christmas. But the gallery show was opening in less than half an hour.

The highlights were Nathan's photos of Zeno the wolf and his pack. It had taken nearly a month for him to track the wolf down. He hadn't been in any of the places Nathan had expected to find him and, out of Lacey's hearing, he'd told Carin he was afraid Zeno, loner that he was, might have died.

In fact, he'd just been too busy to frequent his old stomping ground. The lone wolf was solo no longer. Four young wolf cubs—one who looked remarkably like the young Zeno—were obviously his. A pretty young gray-and-brindle female had made a family man out of him.

"There are some interesting parallels," Gaby said, smiling as she and Stacia hung the show.

"A few," Nathan agreed. He slipped an arm around his daughter and thought how much taller and grown-up she seemed now than last year. Lacey was a teenager, heaven help him. She was talking about boys! He might have to lock her up.

His gaze met his wife's. Everything they'd had the week they met they had again now—only better. They had love. They had trust. They had a future together. They were older, they were wiser. They knew to speak the words the other needed to hear.

"I love you," he mouthed now. "All of you."

All of them. Carin. Lacey. And Joshua, two-month-old Joshua, who—despite the commotion of the opening—was sound asleep in his mother's arms.

Nathan dropped a kiss on his daughter's brow, then leaned in to kiss his wife, a kiss that promised a lifetime of love to the woman he had so nearly lost, and then brushed his lips over his son's downy head.

"The littlest Wolfe cub," he murmured smiling into Carin's eyes.

She smiled back, loving this man now even more than she'd dreamed possible. Loving him for the past, for Lacey. For the present, for Joshua. For the future. Forever.

Their gazes locked.

"But hopefully," she said, "not the last."

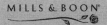

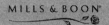

FREE!

2 Books
and a surprise gift!

We would like to take this opportunity to thank you for reading this Mills & Boon® book by offering you the chance to take TWO more specially selected titles from the Modern Romance™ series absolutely FREE! We're also making this offer to introduce you to the benefits of the Reader Service™—

- ★ FREE home delivery
- ★ FREE gifts and competitions
- ★ FREE monthly Newsletter
- ★ Books available before they're in the shops
- ★ Exclusive Reader Service discount

Accepting these FREE books and gift places you under no obligation to buy; you may cancel at any time, even after receiving your free shipment. Simply complete your details below and return the entire page to the address below. *You don't even need a stamp!*

YES! Please send me 2 free Modern Romance books and a surprise gift. I understand that unless you hear from me, I will receive 4 superb new titles every month for just £2.60 each, postage and packing free. I am under no obligation to purchase any books and may cancel my subscription at any time. The free books and gift will be mine to keep in any case.

P3ZEB

Ms/Mrs/Miss/Mr ....Initials ....
BLOCK CAPITALS PLEASE

Surname ....

Address ....

....

....Postcode ....

Send this whole page to:
UK: The Reader Service, FREEPOST CN81, Croydon, CR9 3WZ
EIRE: The Reader Service, PO Box 4546, Kilcock, County Kildare (stamp required)